"You're the last p
see at th

Megan stared at him, dazed. "What are you doing here, Mitch?"

"I came to town on business. I thought I'd come by and see the kids…and you," he added.

His dark brown hair was tousled as usual and a bit of gray showed around the edges. He was looking very fit and handsome. She gave up the pretense. She felt unhinged, and it showed.

"Maybe it would be better if you just left," she said crisply.

"I just wanted to see all of you. I didn't come to cause any trouble, Megan."

Finally her eyes met his. He was intently watching her. In his eyes she saw a sadness that had never been there before.

"I couldn't stay away any longer. It was time to come back," he said softly.

MARTHA MASON

has spent the major portion of her adult life being a stay-at-home mom. Now that her children are grown, she has time to pursue things she has never done before—like writing. "I prayed, asking God what I could do with my time, and unexpectedly I was led to writing. This surprised me, because I never had any aptitude for writing. Composing a note to go on the refrigerator was a major task."

Martha is delighted with writing Christian fiction. Knowing life isn't always perfect, but that things always turn out right if she puts her trust in God. She feels this career change was "inspired." *Two Rings, One Heart* is her first novel. She plans to keep writing, enjoying the new direction her life is taking.

Smith Mountain Lake is where she resides with her husband, Boonie, and her mother-in-law, Beverly. She has three children—Chris, Amy and Andy. With the lake in her backyard, there is always plenty of company. She is also looking forward to the construction of the church she attends. She says the Lord, her family and friends gave her the encouragement she needed to write this book.

Two Rings, One Heart
Martha Mason

Love Inspired®

Published by Steeple Hill Books™

STEEPLE HILL BOOKS

Steeple
Hill™

ISBN 0-373-87045-0

TWO RINGS, ONE HEART

Printed in U.S.A.

And be kind to one another, tenderhearted,
forgiving one another, even as God in Christ
forgave you.

—*Ephesians* 4:32

To "Boonie," Chris, Amy, Andy, Beverly and all my family and friends who believed in me and encouraged me in untold ways. I love you all.

Chapter One

Memories. Old memories, always flooding up from the past. Megan Whitney had built a new life, but the past was always coming to haunt her. Reminders of a life years ago and the husband she had loved and trusted.

Why couldn't she just let it go? Maybe it was because of the kids. But they were a blessing. No, it was deeper than that. It was the promises. The vows she had made to God and to Mitchell.

Megan realized she felt this way every time she had a confrontation challenging her moral values. This time not only had her integrity been questioned, but by the end of the encounter she was being accused of causing her husband's departure. Was it true? Had she been the problem all along?

The day had started out as usual for Megan. She got her two children off to school. Afterwards she opened Meadow Flowers, a once-small florist's shop that she had built into a flourishing nursery and landscape business.

In the morning, she made flower arrangements. After lunch, she delivered them and went to do a final inspection on a landscaping job. From there she went to the high school to pick up her sixteen-year-old son, Zack.

Zack drove his mother to the Division of Motor Vehicles. He was finally old enough to get his driver's license. Coming out of the building, he proudly showed his mother the license. To him it meant freedom to come and go without his mother escorting him. "See Mom, it's official. I can drive now. Aren't you happy?"

"Overjoyed! Now you can do the evening deliveries."

"Aw, Mom!" Zack groaned. "Can I have the truck after that?"

"We'll see," she said, smiling faintly.

The last stop was a meeting to complete a landscape proposal. Megan's day had been hectic, but she didn't complain. There had been lean years in the past, when it had been hard to make ends meet.

Faith in God was her foundation. She had learned to pray, work hard and hold on. Now she no longer had to scrape to make a living. God was faithful.

Zack parked the company van like a pro in front of the newly completed building. Megan grabbed the proposal. "I know you're anxious to try out that new driver's license, but try to wait for me."

Zack grinned wickedly at his mother as he changed the radio station. "Don't be too long or I'll just have to leave you here!"

Inside the building Megan found the owner, Mr. Carlyle, and waited for him to finish a phone conversation. He was a nice-looking man in his mid-fifties. She knew he owned several large properties in the area and was quite wealthy.

Mr. Carlyle glanced over the proposal, wrote a deposit check and handed it to her. They had met on a previous occasion at the work site. She had been in coveralls and had had her hair up in a cap, he recalled.

"Thank you. We'll start work on Monday," she said, then turned to leave.

Mr. Carlyle followed her outside. "Why don't you explain the layout to me one more time?" he said, halting her progress.

Megan pointed out where the trees, shrubs and grass would be planted. "It will be beautiful. I guarantee you'll be satisfied. We also offer lawn care, snow removal and seasonal flower planting. If you're interested, give us a call," she said, handing him her business brochure.

"Ms. Whitney, I think it would be nice if we closed this deal by going out to dinner. To celebrate," he suggested.

"I'm sorry, Mr. Carlyle, I can't. My son is waiting for me," she said politely.

He glanced at the van. "He's a big boy. Drop him at home, change into something nice, and meet me later."

"I also have a little daughter waiting for me to come home and spend some time with her," she said, trying to gently refuse his offer.

"It might be fun," he said, raising his eyebrows.

"Mr. Carlyle, I'm married," she said, glancing at his left hand, seeing that he was wearing a wedding ring.

"So am I. What difference does that make? We're just going out to have a little fun, not make a lifetime commitment," he said laughing.

Megan didn't like the way this conversation was going and she intended to close it. "My crew will start working on Monday, if that suits you?"

As he stared at her without answering, she realized that he was waiting for her to back away or show some sign of submission. When she didn't, he verbally attacked her.

"The way I hear it, your husband hasn't been around for years. And when he was, he was a no-good drunk! Why are you being faithful to him?"

Megan twirled her engagement ring around her finger—something she always did when she was unsettled. Mr. Carlyle was a prominent businessman. He could do her a lot of good, or a lot of harm. *Lord, help me to gracefully extract myself from this situation. Don't let him push it too far.*

"I hear you're an exceptional businesswoman, Ms. Whitney, or may I call you Megan? How are you at negotiations?" he asked, letting her know he was implying more than business.

Megan thought before she spoke. "I have a thriving business."

"Why don't you go out to dinner with me? Maybe we can negotiate another deal," he said suggestively. "You must be lonely and need a little companionship."

"Mr. Carlyle, I'm not sure what you're suggesting, but I have a pretty good idea. I have two children and I believe I need to set an example for them. To go out with you would be inappropriate, since I'm married," she stated.

"Ms. Whitney, there are ways around such concerns. I'm sure your children would understand you going out for a business dinner," he said persuasively.

"Is that all it would be?" Megan asked boldly.

"It can be whatever you want it to be." He grinned smugly. "No one will ever know, but us."

Megan held out the check to him. "Maybe you'd better take this back."

"What's the problem?" He seemed baffled. "We go out and have a little fun. I give you a few good customers. Nobody gets hurt and we all get what we want."

"Doesn't it bother you to break the promises you made to your wife before God?" she asked and waited for him to answer. She honestly wanted to know.

"All that happened a long time ago. We've both changed. And who knows if God is even there or cares?" he said carelessly.

"So you're telling me that the vows you made to your wife and God no longer matter. You're free to do whatever you wish. Who changed the rules?" she asked.

He glared at her angrily.

"You know, if you keep this up, one of these days you're going to go home and she's not going to be there. Maybe you should take your *wife* out to dinner. She may not wait forever," Megan said evenly.

"I don't want to hear this. Especially not from you," he said hotly. "Who are you to preach to me, anyway? You probably ran the poor guy off, after you drove him to drink!"

Megan steadied herself after the assault of cruel words. Then she offered him the deposit check once again.

"No! Keep it. If you're that straight, I know you'll do the job right. Business, you understand," he said sarcastically.

Megan strode to the van quickly, before some of the

harsh words that were reeling through her head could come spewing out. "Let's go home," she said quietly.

Zack started the van. He had watched enough to guess what had transpired. He drove away giving the guy a dirty look.

When they got back to the flower shop, Megan immediately began working. Ted Garrett, her assistant, looked at Zack concerned. He knew Megan always asked how things had been while she was out, or at least said "hi."

"Mr. Carlyle wanted a date," Zack explained, irritated.

"Oh! Did we lose the job?" he asked cheerfully, having worked with Mr. Carlyle types before.

"No! But I nearly lost my cool," Megan said, turning crimson at the thought of the encounter. "He thought I was going to sleep with him!"

"You should have slugged him and told him to keep the job," Ted said, chuckling. "We have enough business without him."

"Don't think that idea didn't cross my mind," she admitted. "We don't get big jobs like that very often. We can't afford to just throw them away. Besides, I know you're looking forward to digging those holes for the trees he ordered," she teased.

By the time they locked the shop, Megan was her usual self again. Zack playfully draped his arm around his mother's shoulder as they walked across the yard to the old farmhouse. "I'm proud of you, Mom. You were something else."

"I'm proud of you, too. I suppose you'll be wanting to take the truck out," she said, pulling out a shiny new set of keys and dangling them before him.

Zack grinned. "How'd you guess?"

"Mothers just know these things," she said, tossing him the keys.

Zack hugged her neck, then dashed inside ahead of her.

"Cool!" said Jess, looking at the picture on her brother's license. "When are you going to take me out?"

When he didn't answer, she turned to her mother. "Gran wants to know if she can pick me up after school tomorrow. We're going shopping and to a movie. Can I spend the night with her?" Jess clamored.

Megan smiled at her daughter's pretty face. To a ten-year-old girl, a trip to the mall with an overindulgent grandmother was heaven. "I guess so."

Zack showed his grandmother his license. She squinted at the picture and smiled at him with approval. "Good job!"

"Thanks for coming over, Ruth," Megan said to her mother-in-law, comforted that Jess hadn't had to stay alone.

Ruth Whitney was in her sixties and retired. She seemed to be at loose ends most of the time. Her husband had died years before. Then Mitchell, her only child, had deserted her as well as his wife and children. Life had been far from perfect for her, but she didn't dwell on that. Megan always included her in all the family activities.

"Mom, my camping trip is tomorrow too!" Zack said anxiously, realizing this would be the first time both he and his sister would be gone overnight at the same time. "I could cancel," he offered, obviously trying not to sound disappointed.

"No way! You guys have been planning this trip for weeks. You're going," she said stubbornly.

Zack knew that was the end of the discussion. His mother had made up her mind. He was a little relieved. He really didn't want to give up the camping trip. Then again he felt a little guilty leaving her alone.

Megan helped Zack load his gear into his friend's father's Jeep the next evening. It was a guys' weekend. Zack didn't get much of that being surrounded by women. "Have a good time!" Megan said, waving as she watched them drive away.

Zack was doing really well for a kid growing up without a father. She tried her best, but sometimes it wasn't enough. There were some things a mother just couldn't do.

With the kids out of the house, it was unusually quiet. Megan found herself at loose ends staring out the window. The farm was mostly gently rolling land, but at the back of the property were foothills into the nearby Blue Ridge Mountains.

She put on some old clothes and started walking down the dirt road that led to the river. She crossed the old wooden footbridge and started climbing the time-worn, rutted-out path. Out of breath when she reached the top, she turned to look back.

The view always made her heart swell, and at the same time humbled her. Below, like a picture, lay her farm. The farmhouse, barns and buildings that made up Meadow Flowers paved their way along the dirt road ending near the river. Each improvement looked as though it belonged, not as though it were an after-thought. Megan had planned it that way from this very spot. It was her favorite place. The kids called it "The Hill."

Megan moved on to an ancient-looking rock and climbed onto it, thinking back to the circumstances that had brought her to this point in her life. The summer she was sixteen, Mrs. Thurlow opened a small flower shop to keep herself busy while her husband farmed. The shop was just a hobby but Mr. Thurlow hired Megan to keep his wife from overworking herself. Megan had just wanted to make a little spending money.

At first the shop had very few customers. Once in a while a friend of Mrs. Thurlow would stop by for fresh flowers to put on the table for dinner guests. Other than that, Megan spent her time pulling weeds, pruning shrubs or helping can vegetables.

Even though she was learning a lot about gardens and plants, she was bored stiff. With her quick mind and lots of time to think, she began coming up with ways to improve business. There was always an excess of fresh vegetables. With the Thurlows' permission, she put a sign near the road advertising homegrown vegetables for sale.

Before long they had a number of regular customers and began getting orders for flowers to be delivered. Mrs. Thurlow had never learned to drive, but Megan had an old car. The two of them would arrange flowers, then set out to deliver them, carrying along a variety of vegetables just in case they could sell some along the way. Usually, they sold everything.

Mrs. Thurlow loved it. She would get to visit her friends, and make a few dollars to boot. Megan also loved it. She was no longer pulling weeds or canning vegetables.

When Megan graduated from high school, Mrs. Thurlow wanted her to work full time and offered her a percentage of what they made. Megan was planning to marry her high-school sweetheart, and needed the job.

By this time, Mrs. Thurlow just wanted to keep her

around. Megan made her feel years younger, the older woman had told her. The delivery trips were like an adventure. Megan always seemed to think up something to keep things interesting. They would stop for ice cream or go by the pond with stale bread and feed the ducks, or ride up to the highest hill just for the view.

Megan had a way with Mr. Thurlow as well. She would bring him a box of jelly doughnuts or pick up the latest trade paper for him. It was his suggestion to give Megan a percentage. He knew she would earn it.

Years later, the Thurlows made the difficult decision to retire and move out west with one of their sons. He had a ranch, and told his dad that he needed help with the chores. They all knew it was because of the health problems that Mr. Thurlow was experiencing. Yet it was the best decision for the couple.

It was bad news for Megan. The young girl that the Thurlows had hired for a summer job was now the mother of two small children and raising them as a single parent. She had no training or experience outside the flower shop. The thought of trying to find a job to support her family was frightening.

The Thurlows were well aware of her situation. They offered to sell her the farm, knowing she loved Meadow Flowers and dreamed of owning it one day. Megan went to her bank and tried to secure a loan. The only collateral she had was her old car and the bedroom furniture Mitchell had given her for their first wedding anniversary. The bank had no interest in either, and turned her down flat. She went to several more banks and loan companies, receiving the same response at each.

With no place else to go, Megan finally turned to God. *Dear God, I don't know what to do. I know, with*

Your help, I can run this business and pay back the money I borrow. If there's any way possible for me to buy this land and if it's Your will, please show me the way. In Jesus' name, amen.

When she got the last negative loan report, she figured it just wasn't meant to be. She braced herself to tell the Thurlows. Parking near the kitchen door of the farmhouse, she knocked on the door.

Mrs. Thurlow answered, smiling. "Megan, this is a surprise!"

"Could I talk to both of you?" she asked seriously.

"Of course, come in," Mrs. Thurlow said, leading her into the family room. "Please sit down."

Mr. Thurlow was reading the paper. Megan nervously waited until she had their full attention. "What can we do for you?" Mr. Thurlow asked, putting the paper down.

Megan sighed. "I just came over to let you know I can't get a loan."

"We were afraid of that," Mrs. Thurlow said sympathetically.

"I wanted to let you know as soon as possible," Megan said, getting up to leave.

"Sit down! We've just been discussing a notion. See what you think of it," Mr. Thurlow said, motioning for her to sit down.

The Thurlows had so many exciting plans. She was really pleased for them, but she wasn't sure she could hear about their unfolding adventure today without crying. Yet out of love and respect for the pair, she put on a happy face and sat back down.

Mrs. Thurlow spoke up first. "You know I've spent all of my life here. Our children have lives of their own. They don't plan to come back here. We hate the thought of developers dividing up the land into housing tracts, but it's a small farm and no one else really wants it.''

Except me! thought Megan.

"You know we have a developer that wants to buy it, don't you?" Mrs. Thurlow asked, then she continued on before Megan could respond. "He wants to cut it up—"

Megan could see Mr. Thurlow was getting impatient with his wife's lengthy story. "What would you think if we loaned you the money?" he blurted out.

Megan's mouth fell open. "I don't understand."

"Well, we would act like the bank. Sell you the place at a decent interest rate. You would make the payments to us. If you can't make a go of it, the farm would come back to us. We'll get a lawyer and do it all legal and business-like," he said, brushing it off and making it sound unimportant. "But we won't need a down payment or any of that stuff. What d'ya think?" Both of the Thurlows were smiling proudly at their idea.

Megan looked from one to the other. She wasn't sure how to take this new turn of events. She didn't want to put Mr. and Mrs. Thurlow in any kind of financial jeopardy. "Are you absolutely sure you want to do this?" she asked, feeling overwhelmed.

"Positive! We checked with a lawyer. He said people do this all the time," Mr. Thurlow said, grinning smugly.

"If this isn't the answer to prayers, I don't know what is," Megan said, smiling bravely. Then she broke down and bawled.

"We know you'll love this place as we have. This is the right thing for you and for us," said Mrs. Thurlow, as Megan wiped her eyes.

Mr. Thurlow stuck out his hand to Megan. "Is it a deal?"

"You better believe it," she replied, grabbing his hand and shaking it heartily.

This was one of Megan's best memories. She thanked God every single day for being so good to her. Her little family thrived on the farm. Meeting the mortgage had been tight in the beginning, but she had found creative ways to meet her payments.

One year, she made pine wreaths and sold them to make the December payment. The next year she put in a pick-your-own pumpkin patch. She always had just enough to pay the bills and give to the Lord.

Megan knew these "patch jobs" weren't going to work forever. She started reading everything she could get her hands on about growing plants. Before long she built a small greenhouse and started her own bedding plants for the coming spring. She planted Christmas trees as part of a long-range plan.

She continued to educate herself. Eventually she offered tree service, snow removal, lawn care and landscaping, along with her florist's service. She even planted bedding flowers in the spring for those who wanted a pretty yard with no bother. She especially enjoyed doing this for older people who really weren't up to digging.

When the time came to hire someone, she prayed, asking God to help her find the right person for the job. Soon she ran into an old high-school friend, Ted Garrett. He was out of work and desperate. He had been a business manager and the store had gone out of business. He had a wife and three little kids.

Ted happened to see Megan at the local building supply store, while picking up a washer for a leaky faucet. "Hi, Megan. How are you doing?" he asked.

"I don't have enough time to do all the jobs that need doing. I'm getting ready to build a retaining wall," she answered distractedly.

"Need help?" he offered.

"I sure do, but everyone's looking for a suit job. They want an office and easy work," she said, thinking he was just making conversation.

That statement hit Ted where he lived. Not knowing he was out of work, she continued on, "I need someone who's willing to put in a hard day's work."

"About what would the job pay?" Ted asked curiously.

"If someone did a good job, more than they would make in an office. For a real hustler, I would be willing to work out a salary-plus-commission job," she said, trying to figure out why he was asking her all these questions.

"What does the job entail?" he asked.

"Being able to keep up with me," she said kidding.

"I can do that," he said cockily. "Consider me."

Megan was surprised. "Why? Are you tired of the retail scene? Or do you want to see what the other half does?" she teased.

Ted looked embarrassed. "No. I lost my job months ago. I haven't been able to find steady work since. All I've looked for is white-collar work, but I need a job and I need it now," he said seriously.

Megan looked away, thinking. *Lord, is this the employee I've been praying for? Show me!* She turned back to Ted. "If you're serious, be at Meadow Flowers tomorrow morning at eight o'clock sharp," she said briskly, and left.

Ted showed up before she got to work the next morning. It had been a hard day, she recalled. She nearly worked him into the ground. He had been working for her ever since. She kept her word; when business grew, so did his paycheck. Ted had definitely been the employee she'd prayed for.

Now Megan had two more full-time employees, and Zack worked part time. Looking back, overall, life had been pretty good. She had few complaints. Though she could use a little more free time…and do without people like Mr. Carlyle.

It always did Megan good to remember her humble beginnings. Her life was in God's hands. She needed to please Him. That was the most important thing.

As the sun began to drop behind the mountains, Megan trekked back down the hill to the farmhouse. It was so empty without the children. She had thought a night by herself might be fun. It wasn't! She found herself wandering from one room to the next as though looking for someone. Finally she went to bed.

Unable to sleep, other memories came into play. Megan began to hear Mr. Carlyle's accusing words. "You probably ran him off…ran him off…ran him off…" She looked at the empty place beside her as the words echoed.

She'd gone over this so many times, but she'd never come to a conclusion. Maybe because she'd never heard Mitchell's side of the story.

She'd been pregnant with Jess. The pregnancy was difficult from the start, kind of like Jess. She had gone to see Doc Crawford for a routine checkup. Her blood pressure had been excessively high. Doc slapped her in the hospital before she had time to argue with him about it.

Once in the hospital, all Megan wanted was to see Mitchell. Ruth had an awful time finding him. He had been fired from his job and hadn't bothered to tell his family. Ruth finally tracked him down at a local bar and drove him straight to the hospital, hoping he would sober up before Megan saw him.

One look at her bleary-eyed husband made her face things she had been refusing to see. He confessed that he had lost his job, blaming it on everyone but himself. Doc pulled him aside and tried to talk some sense into him. Then Ruth drove him home to let him sober up, while she picked up Zack from school.

Later, Mitchell came back to the hospital. He was still in a self-inflicted alcoholic fog. Megan reached for him. "Mitch, what's wrong?"

He came closer and gave her his hand. She took it in both of hers and kissed the palm, then pulled him closer. He looked away, unable to face her.

"Mitchell, I love you," she whispered. She ran her hand through his dirty, tousled hair and down the side of his face, cupping his chin. She waited for their eyes to meet. His were bloodshot and seemed vacant. "We can't go on like this," she said gently. "You need help. Don't you understand? I need help, too," she pleaded, hoping to see some understanding in his eyes.

He shrugged as if it were of little importance. He seemed to want to get away.

His careless attitude caused something in Megan to snap. All the things she had been thinking, but never daring to say, came shooting out. "Mitchell, something is going to change. I will not lose this baby worrying about you. It's time for you to get straight, grow up and accept some responsibility. I need a husband I can depend on. Zack needs a father, not a playmate. When are you going to be there for us, instead of off somewhere with your buddies or lost in a bottle?" Megan began to tear up. "We love you. Why can't you see that?"

She steadied herself. "I know everything seems awful right now, but it will all work out if we just hold on together and trust God to help us."

"When are you coming home?" Mitchell had slurred, ignoring her words.

"In a day or two," said Megan wearily.

"Meg, I never meant for things to get like this," Mitchell finally admitted.

Tears began to run down Megan's face. "I know, but they have."

Mitchell put his head on her chest and let her comfort him. But when Mitchell left, she knew that they hadn't made any progress.

The next evening Mitchell came to visit again. He was on edge and couldn't seem to sit still.

"Mitch, I've made a decision," Megan said evenly. "I'm not sharing you anymore. You have to make a choice which you want more—me and Zack, or drinking. You can't have it both ways. I love you with all my heart, but you're heading down the wrong road and I'm not going with you. I'll help you with anything, but things can't go on the way they are," she said.

She waited for some kind of response. When she got none, she continued. "If you choose the path you're on, we'll have some decisions to make, because one of us is leaving. And know this Mitchell, if you're ever unfaithful to me, it's over. I'll never want to see you again. I want us together as a family. I hope you want that, too." She had stayed strong until she said this. Then she broke down and cried.

Mitchell carefully took her in his arms and held her. "You know I love you, Meg. There's never been anyone else, never will be. I love you and Zack. We'll be okay."

His words had comforted her for the moment, but

the problem had never been other women. It had been alcohol, and nights out with his "ol' buddies."

The next day Megan was released from the hospital. Instead of Mitchell picking her up, Doc drove her home. As soon as she came into the apartment, she knew something was wrong. Zack was there with his grandmother and he rushed into her arms.

Megan turned to Ruth for an explanation and her mother-in-law handed her a note.

Dear Meg,
You're all better off without me. I'm sorry.

I love you,
Mitch

Shattered under the weight of these few words, Megan had collapsed to the floor.

Remembering that day still hurt physically and emotionally. Mitch hadn't even tried to work things out. He'd just packed up and left town. Megan hadn't heard from him since.

Occasionally, Mitchell sent his mother money for the children. Otherwise Megan wouldn't have been sure he was still alive. He never let her know where he was staying or what he was doing. He had cut them all out of his life.

The kids came home after their night away, and life was back to normal.

One afternoon Zack came rushing into the shop after school. "Mom, can I borrow the truck? There's a young adult conference being held at the civic center in Roanoke tonight. Some of my friends and I thought we'd go."

"Why is it in Roanoke?" she asked, disturbed by the distance.

"There's no place here big enough. It's for all the area high-school students. My teachers recommended that we go. They're even offering extra credit to the students who attend. The only catch is that we have to write a one-page report on the conference."

Megan frowned skeptically. She didn't like the idea of Zack driving late at night.

"Come on, Mom, I know it's a forty-five minute drive, but I need the extra credit. It's Friday night, so it won't matter if I'm a little late, will it?"

"What's it all about?" his mother asked grudgingly.

"You should like this! They are supposed to help us understand taking responsibility for ourselves as young adults. They're going to cover a range of subjects like how to handle finances, how to get college aide money, being responsible for moral behavior and substance abuse. It's being sponsored by the area churches," Zack told her.

It sounded pretty good, but Megan was still undecided. "I'm sure they mentioned it before today. Why didn't you tell me sooner?"

"My calculus teacher pulled me aside today and asked me if I was going tonight. I told her no. She said if I would go, she would take my last quiz score off my grade. That would really help me in that class," he admitted.

She knew he was struggling with calculus. "I guess it will be okay," she said reluctantly, wanting to protect him like a mother hen, yet knowing he had to grow up.

"Thanks, Mom!" He gave her a kiss on the cheek and dashed off. Having permission to drive to Roanoke meant more to him than any lectures he and his friends would hear. It made the new driver feel like a big shot.

Megan prayed. It was the only thing she could do. *Lord, I put Zack and his friends in Your hands and ask You to watch over and protect them. In Jesus' name, amen.*

It was after one o'clock before Zack came in that night. Megan was still up reading her Bible, waiting for him. Zack came to the opened door of his mother's bedroom. "I'm home safe and sound," he announced.

"Good, I was about to send out a search party," she teased. "So how was it?"

Zack stared at his mother for a few seconds, then he went to her dresser and fiddled with the things on top. "It really wasn't what I expected at all," he admitted. "They had food and music and all kinds of stuff."

"Well, did you learn anything?" Megan asked, trying to get a little information.

"Yeah, actually I got more than I expected out of going," he said quietly.

Megan frowned. Usually he wanted to tell her everything, word for word. "Were the speakers interesting?" she asked, hoping to draw him out a little.

"It's late. I'll tell you about it another time. Okay?" he said, turning to face her.

"Sure, you can tell me about it tomorrow. I'm glad you're home," she said, but she knew something wasn't right.

Zack walked out mumbling good-night.

"Sleep well!" Megan called, wondering if he and his friends had even gone to the conference. The way he was acting, she suspected they may have gone joyriding instead!

Chapter Two

It was one of those rare afternoons when things were slow at Meadow Flowers. "Why don't you let me close up today?" Ted offered.

"You know, that sounds kind of nice," Megan agreed, knowing Ted was eager for more responsibility. She went home and put a roast in the oven for dinner. Zack was picking up Jess after school.

Megan turned on her "old music," as the kids called it, and stretched out on the sofa. Closing her eyes, she tried to relax.

She was just beginning to unwind when someone knocked on the front door. No one ever came to the front door, except salesmen and uninvited guests. Reluctantly, she got up. Before she could reach the door, another sequence of hard knocks erupted. Somewhat irritated by the visitor's impatience, Megan yanked open the door.

Her uninvited guest watched as the color drained from her face. He threw open the screen when she began to sway, and caught her just before she fell.

The man's touch affected her like a lightning bolt. Megan jerked free, glared at him for a moment, then bolted into the depths of the house. Warily, he followed, and found her draped over the kitchen sink, heaving. Grabbing a towel, he wet it, then put it against her forehead.

Megan shoved him away and buried her face in the wet towel. As she regained a little of her composure, she straightened up.

"Well, you're the last person I expected to see at the door. So...how are you, Mitchell?" Megan said, staring at him with enough anger in her eyes to sear him.

Mitchell looked away, disarmed by her fury. "I've been worse."

"What are you doing here?" she asked, dazed.

"I was in town on business. I thought I'd come by and see the kids...and you," he said hesitantly.

"Well, the children aren't here and you can see I'm not doing too well," she said crisply, as she wiped her face again. "Maybe it would be better if you left."

"I just wanted to see all of you. I didn't come to cause any trouble."

"Just like that, Mitchell! You decide to drop by after ten years! Excuse me for not expecting you!" Her temper flared.

"I was afraid to call. I figured you'd refuse to see me," he admitted.

Megan surveyed the visitor. His dark brown hair was tousled, as usual, with a bit of gray around the edges. He was wearing gray slacks, a white shirt and a red print tie. Not even close to the former dress of this man. He looked very fit and handsome. Her eyes met his.

She looked for signs of alcohol, but saw only sadness. "Why are you back?"

"I couldn't stay away any longer. It was time to come back," he said softly.

"As always, you've only thought of yourself," she snapped. "You come and go when it suits you. You don't give a thought to how it will affect anyone else."

"Is that what you think?" he asked, looking disappointed.

"What else should I think?"

"That maybe I've changed. That I love all of you. That I need to see my family."

"Maybe we don't need to see you. All you'll do at this point is disrupt the children's lives and upset them. We've gotten along fine without you so far."

"I know it seems selfish, but I need to see them," Mitchell said quietly.

"They aren't here. You could stop by again in ten years or so." She lashed out like a whip, and saw him flinch.

Before he could recover, the kitchen door flew open. Zack and Jess came hurrying in. Both stopped short at the sight of the man in the kitchen. Momentarily, Zack stared, then he rushed into his arms. "Dad!" The two held each other tightly, and time seemed to stop.

Jess stood back watching, obviously horrified.

After a long moment, father and son relinquished the hold they had on one another. Mitchell took his son's face in his hands. "I missed you so much!"

"I missed you, too!" Zack exclaimed, tears rising in his eyes.

Mitchell turned to his daughter. "Jessica, I'm your daddy," he said gently.

"Don't you touch me!" Jess said distastefully, giving him a cold stare.

Zack nudged her. "Jess, it's Dad!"

She shook her head, her eyes daring him to come near her.

"Maybe I should go," Mitchell said.

"Why don't you stay for dinner?" Zack asked suddenly.

Now it was Megan's turn to look astonished.

Everyone was unsure how to proceed. Then Jess brought things to a complete standstill. "You're not my father and you never will be." She sneered. Her words had the same effect as a slap across the face. She looked at the hurt expression on Mitchell's face, then ran to her room.

"She didn't mean it, Dad," Zack said, trying to salvage the moment.

"She meant it. I don't blame her for feeling that way. I'm a lousy father," Mitchell admitted, discouraged. He turned to leave.

Zack looked to his mother for help. "Mom!"

Megan couldn't imagine how it would feel to have your child completely reject you. For a moment she felt sorry for Mitchell. Zack was giving her a pleading look. "We have plenty," was all she could think to say. Not exactly an invitation, just a statement of fact.

Mitchell glanced at her. Then he looked at his son.

"Please, Dad. Don't go," Zack begged, flinging himself against his father in a crushing hold.

Megan watched the tender scene, heard them both sniffing. It was too much for her. She slipped out the back door and sat on the steps, trying to grasp the implications of this unannounced visit.

Before long Zack came out and sat beside her. "Mom, please don't be mad."

"I'm not mad at you," she said calmly.

"Can Dad stay for dinner?" he asked.

Megan put herself in Mitchell's place. It was a very grim picture. Zack wanted his father to stay so badly. She touched her son's cheek. "Dinner will be ready soon."

"Thanks, Mom," he said, hugging her and dashing back inside.

A few minutes before Megan put dinner on the table, she went to get Jess from her room. "Dinner is almost ready," she said, entering the bedroom.

"Is he staying?" Jess asked from her prone position across the bed.

"Yes. Zack wanted him to stay," her mother admitted.

"Then I'm not coming down," Jess said defiantly.

"Dinner will be on the table in five minutes. Be there!" Megan ordered, leaving no room for compromise.

She put everything on the table before she called everyone, thinking the less time spent with Mitchell, the better.

Zack came into the kitchen with Mitchell close behind. They sat down in silence. A few minutes passed. Mitchell dared to speak. "Isn't Jessica joining us?"

"She'll be here," Megan stated confidently.

Within seconds Jess came in and took her place. Megan bowed her head and blessed the food. Then they proceeded with the meal without a word.

To break the hush, Mitchell asked Zack, "What subjects are you taking in school?"

Zack seemed relieved to have something to talk

about. "English, Spanish, biology and calculus. I'm doing pretty good, but I'm having a little trouble with calculus," he said, and went on describing his activities.

Jess occasionally peeked at Mitchell, while Megan seemed to be involved in creative food arranging. Time dragged as they waited for a reasonable amount of time to pass. At last the ordeal was over. The dishes were collected and put in the sink.

"May I be excused?" Jess asked, then escaped to her room.

Megan began washing the dishes, glad for something to do.

"Could I give you a hand?" Mitchell offered.

"No. I can do it by myself," she told him quietly.

"Let me show you the farm," Zack said, leading his father outside.

Megan tried to get a grip on herself while they were gone.

When the guys came back twenty minutes later, Mitchell tried to ease the tension. "That was a delicious dinner," he complimented Megan. "You've really got the farm looking great."

"Thank you," Megan said, wiping the counter for the ninth time.

Behind Megan's back, a look passed between the two males. "I have a lot of homework. I guess I better go do it. I'll see you soon, Dad," Zack said, giving his father a hug, then hurrying to his room.

Suddenly Megan found herself alone with Mitchell in a silence that was deafening. She went over to the kitchen door and stood beside it.

Taking the hint, Mitchell started for the door, then

stopped before her. "You look wonderful," he said casually.

"Thanks. Well, I guess we'll see you in another decade or so," she said curtly, letting him know it was past time to go.

"Megan, I'm moving back to Bedford," he divulged.

She stared at him in disbelief. She felt like someone had knocked the air out of her.

"Could I ask you a question?" he asked humbly.

She didn't answer, still stunned by his news.

"Are we still married?" he asked pointedly. When Megan didn't answer, he picked up her left hand. She was wearing the two rings he'd given her years before.

Megan came to herself and jerked her hand free.

"Are we?" he asked gently, insisting on an answer.

"Yes!" Megan shrieked and pushed the screen door open.

"Could we possibly talk sometime?"

"I don't see the purpose. We have nothing to talk about." As soon as he stepped out, she closed and locked the door.

Why did he want to know if they were still married? What was he planning? Why didn't he just stay gone? It would have been easier that way. "Lord, help me," Megan said aloud.

After a restless sleep, Megan woke, hoping the night before had only been a nightmare. But the bad dream had been real.

"Dad looked great, didn't he?" Zack asked cheerfully at breakfast.

Megan studied her son without comment. He'd always dreamed of his dad coming home—his hero.

"Didn't you think he looked good?" Zack pushed for validation.

"He looked fine," Megan admitted.

"He looked like you," Jess said, gawking at Zack. "He's not coming back is he?"

"Who knows?" Megan said with a shrug, trying to dismiss the matter.

"Of course he's coming back," Zack said.

"Don't get your hopes up," Megan warned, clearing the table. All kinds of thoughts started hitting her like arrows from an attacker. Then a missile. What if he were coming back to get a divorce so he could remarry? Maybe after that he would try to get custody of the children! Her head began spinning.

After work, Megan was at the kitchen table mulling over the Mitchell dilemma, when Ruth came in. "Want a cup of coffee?" she asked.

"Thanks. From the way you look, I guess he paid you a visit," Ruth said.

"Yep. Is he staying with you?"

"No! I was shocked to see him. I can't imagine how you feel," Ruth added compassionately.

"Frightened," Megan answered.

"I expected anger or disbelief."

"Oh, they came first. Didn't he tell you?"

"No. He came by my house first. We talked for a while. Then he wanted to know his marital status. I told him he should ask you. Soon after, he left."

Megan's eyes met her mother-in-law's. "He asked me the same question. That's why I'm frightened." Ruth looked puzzled. "What if he came back to get a divorce? Then to get married again. Next he'll want custody of my children!"

"Megan, that's ridiculous. He wouldn't do that," Ruth said calmly.

"How do you know? He's been gone ten years. We don't know what he's like anymore!" She knew she was beginning to sound hysterical.

"He just wants to see his family," Ruth said soothingly.

"You're his mother. A mother never gives up."

"Have you given up? Has he been gone too long?"

"I don't know," she said thoughtfully. "I opened the front door and it was like looking at a ghost. I've never felt so unhinged. He just stood there staring at me. I thought maybe he wasn't real. I'm not ready for this."

"When do you think you will be?" Ruth looked at her hopefully.

"I don't know. Maybe never," Megan said angrily.

Ruth sipped her coffee. "How did last night go?"

"Well, I almost fainted. Then I threw up. After that the kids came home. Zack was thrilled and invited him to stay for dinner. Jess glared at him like he was an ax murderer. And I was…brittle."

"Sounds like a fun evening." Ruth chuckled. "When's he coming back?"

"I have no idea." Megan stared into her coffee cup.

"You know he's going to want to see the kids."

"I don't have to let him. He has no part in their lives!" she said defensively.

"No, you don't. But if he really wants to see them, he can go to court," she replied realistically. "Why don't you consider letting him see them for a couple of hours at a time. Zack's a big boy, he'll watch out for Jess."

"Did he ask you to come over here?" Megan asked suspiciously.

"No, but I'm caught in the middle anyway. It's not like they're babies and he could run off with them. If he tried that with Jess, you know he'd be bringing her back in short order when *she* got through with him."

Megan laughed at the thought. Then the kids came in and the entire conversation was about Mitchell.

Megan went out to the porch swing. She hadn't thought of anything else all day. She couldn't take any more.

Later, Ruth came out to tell her goodbye. "Are you all right?" she asked. Megan shrugged. "You know, you'll never find out if he's changed if you don't give him a chance," Ruth said.

"I'll pray about it," Megan replied.

Ruth sat down beside her and gave her a long, soothing hug. "I can't help it, Megan. He's my son. I love him."

"I know," Megan said.

Ruth left, pondering all the problems. She had grown up in hard times. Her parents had worked themselves into early graves. Her siblings were spread over the country and she seldom saw them. The mainstays in her life were God and her family. When her husband died and her son disappeared, she didn't know where to turn. God was her answer. She could do little now for her loved ones, other than to pray for them.

Thursday night after dinner, the children went to their monthly school skate. Megan was looking forward to the time alone. Before she could settle down, there was a knock on the front door. Once again she found Mitchell standing outside.

"You're not going to faint this time are you?" he teased.

"No," Megan snapped. "The children are out." She started closing the door.

"I know. That's why I came by. We need to talk about them," he said.

Megan stopped short, knowing Ruth—her friend, his mother—had told him she would be alone.

"May I come in? Please?"

He didn't sound demanding, only hopeful. Something in his humble attitude caused her to relent. She opened the door and led him to the formal dining room, deciding the tone of this meeting would be businesslike. As they sat down across the table from one another, their eyes met. Megan raised her head and stuck out her chin.

"You don't want me to see them at all, do you?" Mitchell asked patiently.

"Not really," she replied with cold, hard honesty.

"Would you rather we go through the courts?" he asked.

"No!" Megan had been to that madhouse with business problems. She wasn't about to trust them with her children.

"Can we come to an agreement?" he asked, never taking his eyes off her.

"I'll consider letting you see them, as long as you follow certain conditions," she said in a strained voice.

"Such as?"

"There will be absolutely no drinking. If there is, don't ever ask to see them again," she ordered staunchly.

"I don't drink anymore," he said, without looking away.

Megan was taken aback, but she continued on. "No overnight visits. If you take them out, both go. I'll want to know where you're going, what you'll be doing…and no one else goes along," she ordered.

He frowned at the last one. "What do you mean, no one goes along?"

"I don't want girlfriends or 'ol' buddies' or whatever going along. If you can't spend time with the children alone, then don't bother," she said emphatically.

"No problem," he responded seriously. Then his tone softened. "Could I ask one favor?" Megan waited without responding; she wasn't going to give him any help. Mitchell took a deep breath. "Would you give me a little help with Jessica?"

Megan rubbed her temples, considering his request. Jess was ready to reject him and forget it. Megan almost welcomed the idea. She knew it wasn't right to turn Jess against her father. She'd never done it before. Was she going to start now? She looked across the table at Mitch. "All right, but don't expect too much from her." She sighed.

"I understand. Could I possibly take the kids out this weekend?" he asked.

"I'll have to think about it. Call me on Saturday," she said, and stood up. The meeting was over.

Mitchell followed her to the door and stopped. "You've been more generous than I deserve. Thank you," he said gratefully.

"Don't disappoint my children!" she warned, holding the screen door open.

Megan immediately closed the door and leaned against it. Why did his visits rattle her so? And how was she going to be able to let him see her kids?

She was the one who had always been there for them. The one who had spent sleepless nights taking care of them. The one who was there for the plays and programs, who bandaged the cuts and scrapes. The one with them when they were sad or lonely or scared or just out of sorts. The one who helped them with their homework, buried their pets, and saw them through disappointments. Now, ten years later, Mitchell wanted to reappear and be their daddy. Where was he when they needed him? Where was he when *she* needed him?

Unsettled after Mitchell's visit, Megan needed to get out of the house. She wandered down the road to the river. On her way, she had visions of Zack and Jess, at earlier ages, scampering ahead of her. They had traveled this way together often.

It was wonderful watching her children romp and play as they were growing up. In the winter they would sleigh ride on the hills and build snowmen. In the spring they would pick wild flowers and watch the land come to life. In the summer they would swim in the river and go fishing. In the fall they would climb the foothills into the mountains and camp out once in a while.

Megan sat down on the riverbank. She would never forget those times, but it would never be like that again. In a couple of years, Zack would be leaving for college. Jess was already getting involved in school and spending time with her friends. Now they'd be fitting ''daddy'' in their time, too. She imagined herself last on the list—lonely and forgotten.

Megan felt tears as she thought of what the future might hold. *Why did he have to come back? Why, God? We've made it this far without him. Why is he back?*

Megan looked around at her farm. Why did Mitchell

make her feel so insecure? She had two wonderful children and a successful business. She had no right to complain. She could kick herself for giving in to self-pity.

Her thoughts turned to Mitchell. Visions of homeless men, drunks staggering around in a stupor, living in alleys and digging through Dumpsters for food, flashed through her mind. She shuddered.

Over the years, she had wondered how Mitchell looked. Now she knew. The straight nose was somewhat crooked. The unruly hair hadn't changed much. The strong jaw seemed as determined as ever. The eyes were where she saw a change. They were no longer blank and empty, but peaceful—yet sad. He used to be unable to look her in the eye. Now he stared without flinching. That flustered her and put her on the defensive.

She thought back over her conversation with him. If she'd told him he could only see the children for five minutes once a year, he probably would have accepted. It made her so sad to think of the scraps he'd settle for, when he could have had it all.

All the land before her eyes could have been theirs. *I'll never understand how he just gave up his family. I'm tired of being haunted by regrets and guilt. I was the best wife I knew how to be. If that wasn't enough, I'm sorry.*

Early Saturday morning the phone rang. Megan let it ring a few times before answering it, afraid it was Mitchell.

"What did you decide?" he asked as soon as he heard her voice.

"You can pick them up at one today and take them

out for a couple of hours," she said reluctantly. "We'll see how it goes. Where do you plan to take them?"

"To play putt-putt golf, or we'll go roller skating if that suits you," he said eagerly.

"Either is fine. Things better go right," she warned and hung up.

When she told the kids, Zack was ready to go. Jess was infuriated. "I don't want to go out with him! I don't know him. I won't go!" she insisted and started to stomp out.

"Both of you will go out with your father this afternoon," Megan said firmly.

"Mom!" Jess pleaded. "I don't want to go."

"Jess, he's your father. You should at least give him a chance," she reasoned.

"Why? He never bothered to notice I was alive. He's not my father. He's just some guy that showed up the other night that I don't know!" Jess shouted.

Megan stared at her calmly. She had expected this. "This will give you a chance to get to know him. He's picking both of you up at one. Be ready."

"Thanks a lot, Mom!" Jess shouted and ran to her room.

"Well, that went better than I expected," Zack commented sarcastically.

Megan flashed him an unsteady smile. He had always been the easy child. Jessica had fought from the day she was born. She never went along with the plan. Megan had learned simply to put her foot down and to end the discussion.

This time, Jess was right. Her father *was* a stranger. Megan had given Mitchell her word to give Jess a little push in his direction. If this visit didn't go well, she would push no more.

Megan left Jess in her room, sulking, and went to work feeling guilty.

At twelve o'clock she locked the shop and walked home with Zack. He was also feeling unsettled. "Mom, nothing will ever come between us. But sometimes…I need Dad." He almost sounded as though he was apologizing.

"I told him I would let him see you, but if anything isn't right, I expect you to tell me. If anything happens that shouldn't, I'll come and get you," she said firmly.

"Mom, nothing will happen," he assured her.

"Zack, the last time you saw your father, you were a little boy. He wasn't like he seemed to you. He had problems, big problems. He may still have them. If he does, I don't want either one of you with him. Do you understand?"

Zack nodded, but she could tell he was itching to argue on his father's behalf.

Just before one, Megan went to see if Jess was ready. She felt like she was pushing her daughter into the lion's den, but she found Jess sitting on her bed, waiting patiently, with her frilliest dress on. Megan reconsidered. Maybe it was Mitchell she should be feeling sorry for.

It was exactly one when Mitchell pulled in the driveway. Megan watched from the door as Zack and Jess climbed into the strange car. It drove away. But somewhere in her heart, she knew they would be back by three safe and sound.

Actually, they were back five minutes early. Mitchell evidently wasn't taking any chances on getting on Megan's wrong side again.

Jess came flying in the door and headed straight for

her room. "Is everything all right?" Megan asked as Zack came in.

"Yeah. Great! We went to play putt-putt golf. Jess seemed to have a good time, but she'd never admit it. Dad's out on the porch. He wants to talk to you," he said, looking hopeful.

Megan went charging out the door, then stopped short when she found Mitchell perched on the porch railing in a familiar pose.

Memories seemed to have overcome Mitchell as he looked off into the distance. He appeared to snap back to reality at the irritated edge to Megan's voice. "Zack said you wanted to talk to me."

"I thought I'd let you know today went pretty well, thanks to you," he admitted.

Megan didn't know what to say. "Did Jess give you a hard time?"

"She was a little icy." He grimaced.

"Then you fared well. I had to force her to go. By the way, *she* picked the outfit."

He laughed. "I wondered about that." Another uncomfortable silence followed. "Look, I just wanted to tell you, I didn't come back to cause trouble or hurt anyone. I just want to get to know my kids. I've missed enough already."

Why? Megan wondered. *After all this time, why did you bother to come back?* Instead she said, "I hope life is better for you now than it was when you left."

"Much better. Thank God," he said easily.

"I'm glad," she said, turning to go into the house.

"Could I possibly take them out again tomorrow?" he asked quickly.

"We go to church." It was the only thing she could think of to say.

"Later in the afternoon maybe?"

"Two, back by five," Megan ordered officially.

"Yes, ma'am," he said, teasingly.

She glared at him. "Where do you plan on going?"

"To a movie or roller skating—depending on how Jess dresses."

"Fine," she said, turning to go in. He was learning fast. He already had it covered no matter how Jess dressed.

"See ya," Mitchell called after her. Like old times.

Megan heard him, but she chose not to respond. Feeling in her heart that old empty ache of love gone wrong. "'Bye, Mitch," she whispered to herself.

Inside Zack was waiting to ambush her, wanting to tell her all about the afternoon. "Mom, it was so great! Dad said…Dad did…Dad likes…" He went on and on as Megan listened patiently.

"He asked if he could see you both again tomorrow," she added, when he took a breath.

"You told him yes, didn't you?"

"He's picking you up at two."

Jess was coming down the stairs and overheard them talking. She rushed into the room. "Oh no, not again. I'm not going out with *him!*" she roared.

"Ah, Jess, you know you had a good time today," Zack said. "Stop acting like such a baby!"

"What's the problem, Jess?" Megan asked, feeling guilty for forcing her.

Her daughter shrugged and made a face. "I don't know."

"So, nothing's really wrong. You just don't want to go. Right?"

"Mom," she began to whine, but the look on her mother's face told her it was a waste of time.

"I believe you need to at least give him a chance. Don't you?" Megan asked.

Jess nodded slightly.

The next morning at church, Megan heard little of the service. She was too busy asking God why, then not listening for His reply.

That afternoon Mitchell took the children roller skating. He felt that was safe, since Jess came out in jeans that looked well worn. Unbeknownst to him, skating was one of her favorite pastimes.

Jess had decided ahead of time that this wasn't going to be any fun. When there was a couples skate, she refused to skate with Mitchell. Zack went off with a girl he knew from school.

Later, she fell skating. When Mitchell rushed to help her, she shrieked, "Leave me alone!" loud enough to turn a few heads in their direction. From then on, she made him as miserable as possible. He ended up bringing them home early.

"Come on in, I want you to see my science project," Zack said, dragging his reluctant father inside.

Megan was nowhere in sight, so Jess began searching for her. She found her on the swing on the back porch. "Mom, I fell and hurt my leg really bad," Jess moaned as she limped over.

"Let me see," Megan said, making room beside her.

Jess sat down and pulled up the leg of her pants. Then she stuck her leg in her mother's face for her to examine closely.

"Oh! You really bruised that, didn't you," Megan said, knowing Jess wanted sympathy, even though there was hardly a mark.

"It hurts a lot. I wanted to come home, but *he* made me stay," she said pitifully.

Megan grabbed Jess and hugged her firmly. "You know something?"

"What?" Jess growled.

"I love you," Megan giggled and gave Jess a kiss.

Jess wasn't giving up yet. "I missed you. I kept thinking about you here all alone. Maybe next time Zack could go and I could keep you company."

"I was fine. I got some reading done." Megan held up her book.

Jess was trying to figure out her next maneuver, when Mitchell came out the door. "I just wanted to tell you goodbye," he said quietly.

"I was showing Mommy my leg," she said, glaring at him accusingly.

"I'm sorry you got hurt," he said.

Jess was having none of it. She got out of the swing and started to march inside, then remembered to limp.

Megan saw Mitchell's bewildered expression. "Hold it, young lady! Don't you have something to say?"

Jess swallowed her arrogant attitude. "Thank you for taking us skating," she said, then quickly escaped.

Mitchell watched until she was inside. Then he turned his attention to Megan, who had a frown on her face. "What?" he asked, confused.

"She really has you hopping," Megan commented.

"She hates me. She as much as told me so."

"She still might. She's no angel. She may look like one, but inside beats the heart of a true cynic, or so she'd like us to believe," Megan said knowingly.

"You're very smug," he said.

"Well, if she keeps this up, you'll be dancing to her tune. That will suit her fine."

"I'll call about the next time," he said, flustered, and started off the porch.

"After two visits are you running scared?" she asked haughtily.

He turned back to face her. "You know, I never remember you being spiteful!"

"I never remember you being a coward!"

"A coward!" he said, amazed by the accusation.

"You're having second thoughts because a child you neglected for ten years hasn't taken to you right away! If you're truly interested in a relationship with your daughter, it will take more than two afternoons of fun and games. You're the one who came back and started this. So don't blame Jess! Make up your mind if you really want to be a father, because neither one of them needs to be hurt again," she said bitterly.

Megan's words stung. Jess wasn't like Zack, who was ready to welcome him home. Jess wanted nothing to do with him. His shoulders sagged as he thought of what he would have to face to build a relationship with her.

Megan noted his defeated look. "Look, she doesn't want a father or a mother or a grandmother or anyone else telling her what to do or how to do it. It's not just you."

Mitchell looked perplexed. "Why are you telling me this?"

"Because I know Jess. She's a pro, you're not. She's made *teachers* cry. She has this knack for making people feel guilty and unworthy, and she does it well. Most of it's a facade—she's really a sweetheart underneath. Don't give up on her too easily. She's worth the effort." Megan's expression softened.

Mitchell leaned against the porch railing. "I apologize for calling you spiteful."

"Don't make any rash decisions," she warned.

"Do you still consider me a coward?"

She raised her eyebrows. "We'll see."

"I'll be out of town on business for the next week. That's why I said I'd call about the next visit," he explained. "If you should need to get in touch with me for any reason, call See Life. They'll know how to locate me."

"Lucky them. We'll manage," she added dryly.

"How well I know you can manage alone. I'm reminded of that fact every time I come out here. Regardless, if an emergency comes up, call me. Please."

Megan shrugged. "If that's what you want. Who should I call, Sea Fish?"

"See Life," he repeated. "It should be a new listing." He started to leave, then he turned back to enlighten her a bit. "You know Jess gets it from you."

"Not all of it," Megan said, giving him a look that made him realize he was on shaky ground. She picked up her book, letting him know he could leave now.

"I'll call while I'm gone," he repeated.

"Suit yourself," Megan answered without looking up. Thank goodness she wouldn't have to deal with him for a few days. Maybe he wouldn't bother to come back.

"See ya," Mitchell said quietly, and left.

Chapter Three

Megan relaxed a little with Mitchell out of town. Then she began thinking. Maybe he had left again for good. She decided to call Sea Weed, or whatever, to see if he had been telling her the truth.

She dialed information. "I'd like a new listing, Sea something-or-other."

The operator gave her the information and she punched in the numbers. "See Life. May I help you?" a friendly female voice asked.

"Yes. Do you have a Mitchell Whitney employed there?" she asked.

"Oh, yes. But Mr. Whitney is out of town. Could I take a message?"

"Could you possibly tell me Mr. Whitney's position?"

"Well, Mr. Whitney handles everything. Could I tell him who's calling?" she asked.

"No, thank you," Megan said, hanging up. So he had a job. Big deal.

* * *

On Monday morning, Megan cheerfully answered the phone. "Meadow Flowers. How can I help you?"

"You could tell me you missed me," Mitchell said timidly.

"I didn't know you'd be back so soon," she replied indifferently.

"I missed you guys," he admitted anyway. "Would it be possible for me to see the kids tonight?"

"It's not a good idea for them to be out late on school nights," she said, trying to put him off. Just hearing his voice, she was tensing up again.

"We'll go out for pizza and a quick trip to the mall, and be home by seven," he persisted.

Megan thought of Zack. He'd been waiting all week to see his father. "They get home around 3:45. I'll leave a note saying you'll pick them up at four."

"Would you care to join us?" he asked, then waited through a long silence.

"I have to work late," she said, and hung up.

With the kids out of the house, Megan again began thinking of the past. Everything had been wonderful the first few years. She and Mitchell had gotten married right out of high school. A couple of years later, Zack had been born. Mitchell was beside her through everything. Mitch would get up with her to feed Zack. Then they would stand by his crib and watch him sleep. If something had been wrong with the relationship, she hadn't seen it.

Later Mitch wasn't happy with his job. They saved for him to go to night school, but as soon as he started, one thing or another went wrong. Mitch started going out with some of the guys after work to commiserate over a few beers.

It wasn't long before Mitchell was missing some of his classes and neglecting to study. He began making careless mistakes at work, then not showing up for work. He didn't show up for work one time too many. They fired him.

His father put the pressure on him and told him to shape up. Everything was fine for a while. Things were going well, except that he was still meeting the "ol' buddies" every now and then.

Then without warning, Mitchell's father died. The two of them had been really close, and Mitchell took his father's death hard. No longer was the man he loved and respected there to jerk him up short when he needed it.

It was about that time that Mitchell began spending his weekends drinking with "the guys." Everything started to add up again. Only this time he began pulling into himself and away from his family. But all that was the past. Megan didn't want to think about it anymore. She went to wash clothes to keep occupied.

She was in her room, reading, when the kids came home. Jess dashed in with a shopping bag in hand and flopped down beside her. "Look what I got!" she exclaimed excitedly, pulling out a pair of dress boots.

Megan had seen them before, when she told Jess they were too expensive and looked too old for her. "You talked your dad into buying them?"

"He thought they were pretty and he didn't mind getting them for me," Jess jabbered.

Then Zack came in carrying a shopping bag. He showed his mother two pairs of jeans and a nice sweatshirt. "Dad got some jeans and a shirt. He wanted to buy us something," he explained in an apologetic tone.

"That was nice of him," Megan said.

"Mom, he asks about you every time we go out," Zack said.

"I've got homework," Jess said, obviously bored. She seemed disappointed that her mother hadn't gotten mad at her dad for buying the boots. Hadn't made him take them back.

"Mom, you could be a little nicer to him," Zack pushed.

"Zack, go do your homework!"

"Mom, we used to be so happy. It could be that way again."

Megan got up. "I need to see if the doors are locked."

"I locked them when we came in," said Zack, and continued to badger her. "You always told us everyone deserves a second chance. Why doesn't that pertain to Dad?"

She stopped short. "You don't know what you're talking about. I gave him chance after chance after chance. Face it, Zack, he chose alcohol over us."

"He was drinking then. He's not now. He's changed."

Megan stared at her son, unmoved.

"Give him another chance. You'd do that for a stranger," he pointed out.

It was ironic that Zack was defending his father to her. "You just don't understand, Zack. He broke my trust in him. He just walked away and never even got in touch with me. He broke my heart," she added.

"But he came back!" he argued.

"Too late."

"Only because you won't give him a chance."

Megan's mouth gaped opened. It took her a few seconds to pull herself together. "I didn't leave. *He* did," she said quietly.

The next morning Megan was sipping a cup of coffee, when Zack came downstairs.

"I'm sorry about last night," Zack admitted stiffly.

"I'm glad your dad is back for you. Can't you accept that and be happy?"

"I still think you two should at least try to be friends. If for no other reason than for Jess and me. We need parents who aren't at each other's throats," he said dryly.

"I'll think about what you said," Megan conceded.

"Dad wants us to go out with him for dinner Wednesday night."

Megan nodded that she heard him, but said nothing.

Wednesday night Megan fixed a snack, turned on the radio to her favorite oldies station, and sat at the kitchen table to do some book work. Right at seven, the children came in.

"Mom, do you mind if Dad and I watch the game here?" Zack asked, his displeasure with her still showing. "If you do, we can go to his place."

"Here is fine," Megan answered quickly, knowing Zack was testing her. The last thing she wanted was her son hanging out at Mitchell's place.

Mitchell had refused to come in until Zack got permission. As they came through the kitchen, Mitchell spoke, Megan nodded.

Later, Megan heard Jess in the family room with them. She shook her head in amazement. Jess put up such a front that she hated Mitchell.

When the game was over, Zack made his exit before

Mitchell reached the kitchen. "'Night, Dad," he said, and dashed up the stairs.

"We'll do something this weekend," Mitchell called after him.

Megan grumbled and started erasing frantically.

"Problems?" Mitchell asked.

Megan dropped the pencil and began to rub her temples. "I've been at it too long. All the numbers keep coming up wrong," she confessed.

He peeped over her shoulder. "Maybe I could help?"

Megan knew he was good in math, and she was tired. She slid the adding machine over to the next chair.

Mitch ran up the figures twice. Then he rechecked his numbers against hers. "You transposed some numbers," he said, showing her.

Megan leaned back in the chair. "Numbers never were my thing."

"I remember."

She got up. "Want some coffee?"

"Would you mind?" he asked.

"No. I wanted to ask how things were going." She poured him a cup and added one sugar. When she realized what she had done, she glanced at him, hoping he hadn't noticed. He was grinning at her. She dumped in another sugar. "So, how are things?" she asked casually, handing him the cup.

"I'm not sure," he admitted.

Megan propped her head on her hands. "You're doing okay."

"How do you know?" he asked, frowning.

She smiled. "Because Jess doesn't like to watch sports on TV."

Mitchell looked surprised. "Thanks. I needed to hear that."

Their eyes caught in uncertainty. Megan felt her expression turn from smiling and happy to clouded and sad. Then her eyes became watery and she dropped her head between her arms for a moment.

"Thanks for the help," she said, lifting her head, her composure regained.

Mitchell got to his feet. "I better get going. Thanks for the coffee." Neither had touched it.

Walking back to his car, Mitchell wondered what was going through Megan's mind. So many times she had been willing to help him. And instead of accepting, what had he done? Thrown all of her caring and love back in her face by leaving her. He had been such a fool. He had made a lot of mistakes. He couldn't just forget them. He had to try to right them. And it might take him a long time. He needed to find a place where they could begin again.

As the longer days of spring arrived, Megan's busy season began, and working late became the norm.

The kids barely noticed. Zack gave up time with his friends to be with his father. Jess was enjoying all the benefits, but still being a brat.

Ruth saw her son on a regular basis. Most of the time he came over to cut the grass or take care of some other job that needed doing. She figured that he was trying to make up for the past.

When Megan's sister, Cass, heard Mitchell was back, she wasted no time before calling. Cass never had anything good to say about Mitchell. She felt her sister had married the wrong man. She always held up her extravagant life to Megan as an example to strive for. As soon as Megan answered the phone, Cass started right in.

"Megan, I heard Mitchell's back in town. I certainly hope you're keeping Jessica and Zachary away from him!"

"Hi, Cass. How are you?" Megan asked, ignoring her sister's comment.

"Why didn't you tell me? You're letting him see them, aren't you!" she accused. "You know you really have no sense at all when it comes to that man. He has no right to see them. He deserted you! Tell him he can do you a favor and get lost for the rest of your life. Then maybe you can start living again!"

"Cass, Mitchell is and always will be the children's father. That's all there is to it."

"From my standpoint, he has no rights at all. He gave them up when he walked out on you." Then a new thought came to Cass. "You'll be the one he wants to see next. Then what?" She waited only a second before she started in again. "I'll tell you what will happen. He'll move in with you. Then he'll take over your business and ruin that for you. Then you and the children can be penniless again when he takes off to who-knows-where. Megan, wake up! The man's no good. You were just too young and naive to see it before. Surely you've smartened up a little over the years."

"I've got to go, Cass. Talk to you soon," Megan said, and hung up.

But Cass just couldn't leave it alone. She called their parents and got them all stirred up. Before the night was over, they called Megan.

"Megan, what on earth is going on there? Cass is frantic. She says Mitch is back and up to his old tricks again!'' her father bellowed as soon as she answered the phone.

"Dad, he moved back to Bedford. I had nothing to do with it."

"I can't believe you're letting him see the children. What right does he have? He could get Zack involved in the wrong things. And how is poor Jess? I'm sure she's horrified by all this. How could you, Megan?" he raged.

Then her mother got on the phone. "Megan, why are you letting him see the children?" she asked a little more gently.

"Mom, Zack is sixteen and he wants to see his father. If I forbid him, I'll be forcing him to go behind my back. He loves his father. Jess is another matter. I'm doing the best I know, and that's all I can do."

"Megan, it's your job to protect them. They're only children. Zack is still impressionable. Mitchell could sway him the wrong way. And it's not fair to force Jess to get to know a man who never cared for her."

"Mom, I know this is a very emotional issue for both of you, it is for me too. But I have to do what I think is best."

"Well, you've taken a big risk with your children's futures. I hope you know that. Use your head instead of your heart," her mother advised.

When she got a chance, she told them goodbye and hung up.

The entire week had gone like that. Everyone was so good at giving her advice. But no one had been there to help after Mitchell left, except Ruth and Doc. Cass had been too busy with her social life. Her parents had been in the process of retiring and moving to Florida. Her friends had had their own problems.

It was the same all over again. Everyone had something to say and they expected Megan to take their advice. She was weary from defending herself. Zack was encouraging her to spend time with Mitchell and give him a chance to prove himself.

Jess was in a class all by herself. She managed to find ways to make her mother feel guilty about making her see her father. That was Jess.

One evening, Megan came dragging home from work. Mitchell was planning to take the kids out to dinner. She figured she would stay in her room until they left. She was halfway up the stairs when someone knocked on the front door. It was too early for Mitchell, and besides, he had finally learned to use the kitchen door. Who on earth could it be? She retraced her steps and opened the door. Mitchell was standing there, looking nervous.

"The kids aren't quite ready yet," she said, motioning for him to come in.

"Good. I wanted to talk to you first," he said, looking anywhere but at her.

"Is anything wrong?" she asked concerned.

"No. I just wanted to ask you something without them around," he said, shuffling from one foot to the other.

Before he could get to the point, the kids came rushing down the stairs. Zack came to a halt when he saw a wrapped box in his father's hand.

"Would both of you wait for me in the other room?" Mitchell requested.

"Sure," Zack answered, hauling Jess along with him.

"Why? What's going on?" Jess's radar was up, then she saw the box. She let Zack lead her to just inside the kitchen. Then she abruptly stopped, and shushed her brother so she could listen.

Megan stood before Mitchell with her shoulders slumped and her head down, waiting for bad news. She hadn't even noticed the box. He handed it to her. "For me?" she asked stunned and gingerly took it.

He smiled weakly. "It's candy. I figure you have enough flowers."

"Why are you giving me a gift?" she asked, suddenly feeling like crying.

"Meg…will you go out with me?" he pleaded.

Her head snapped up. "Wh-what?"

"I'm asking you to go out with me—on a date," he admitted tensely.

Her eyes searched his. Was this some sort of joke? The look on his face told her it wasn't. She was about to refuse, when Jess came bolting into the foyer.

"A date!" she screeched, fighting Zack off as she made her way to her mother. "Mom, you can't go on a date!" she ordered, pulling her mother to face her. "You're too old. I won't let you go out with him!" she shrieked.

That did it. Megan had absolutely had enough of everyone telling her what to do. She glared at Jessica, who had just reminded her that she was almost as old as she felt. She turned back to Mitchell. "Exactly what did you have in mind?" she snapped.

"Dinner and a movie," he said quickly, knowing she was about to explode. "A nice restaurant with real menus and tablecloths. No fast food. Then a buy-a-ticket, fresh-popcorn-type movie."

"When?"

"Saturday night?" he sputtered.

"Fine," Megan said, taking the box of candy and marching up the stairs without another word. Hot with anger she reached her room and flung the box of candy on the bed. She'd really sunk to a new low when a ten-year-old thought she could tell her what she could and couldn't do. She was tired of everyone telling her how to run her life. She stomped around her room several times muttering to herself. "I don't need Jess or Zack or anyone else telling me what to do." It was then she realized that she had just told Mitchell she would go out with him! How could she be so stupid?

She spun around and dashed out of her room and back down the stairs. She ripped opened the front door, just in time to see the taillights disappear down the road.

Wearily she climbed the stairs. Maybe if she took a hot bath, it would stop her head from throbbing.

She stayed in the tub until she was wrinkled like a prune, but it didn't help much. Wrapped in her robe, she flopped across the bed, noticing a card attached to the box. She slowly opened it. *Meg, please give me a chance. Mitch.*

Exasperated, she tore open the candy and stuffed a piece in her mouth. How did he manage to ask her out when her guard was down? If Jess hadn't come rushing in giving her orders, she would have said no!

She got up, popping another piece of candy in her mouth. She went over to the dresser and opened the drawer that held her special treasures. She dug around until she found a box with pictures, then began sifting through them.

Megan found the picture of her first date with Mitchell. They had been on their way to a school dance. She touched his face in the picture.

She sat on the bed, remembering that night. Mitch had been so sweet. He had brought her a single, red rose. When he looked in her eyes, she had gone weak in the knees. When they slow danced, he sang to her.

After the dance, he drove her straight home. At the door, he asked if he could kiss her good-night. She sighed as she remembered. He had gently taken her face in his hands and, looking in her eyes, he had kissed her ever so softly.

From that night on they never dated anyone else. He was always gentle and considerate, never rushing their relationship. Treating her as though she was precious.

She pulled herself back to the present. Tomorrow she would call him and back out.

Every day Megan intended to call Mitchell and cancel the date, but each time something would come up to stop her. Friday night she had every intention of talking to Mitchell when he brought the kids home. But she fell asleep on the sofa instead, and didn't wake up until he had driven away.

Saturday morning, with butterflies in her stomach, she called the number Zack had given her. There was no answer. She tried again later in the day. There was still no answer. At four o'clock she called again.

Mitchell answered on the second ring. "Hello."

Megan went mute. She listened to his deep, familiar voice say "hello" three times before she pressed the disconnect button.

She stood frozen with the dead phone in her hand for several minutes. She couldn't believe she had done that.

Chapter Four

Zack offered to stay with Jess on Saturday night. His mother hadn't given him an answer. He decided he wasn't going to make any plans, just in case she didn't chicken out. At five o'clock Saturday night she still hadn't said anything. He decided to go to her room, where she'd been hiding out all afternoon, and ask.

As he came to the door, she was in the adjoining bathroom drying her hair. When she noticed him, she looked a little uneasy. "Mom, are you going out to-night?" he asked, trying to make it sound as though it wasn't any big deal.

"I guess I am. Are you still offering to stay with Jess?" she asked, trying to look calm.

"Sure, I told you I'd stay with her," he said, trying not to grin.

"Jess isn't going to like this!"

"Maybe not, but I do," he said honestly.

"Then get out of here and let me get ready," she said nervously.

Zack answered the front door when his father arrived

and checked him over. Mitchell was neatly dressed in a navy sport coat, blue shirt, gray slacks and a print tie. "You look great," said Zack, nodding his approval.

Mitchell tugged at his collar, looking like he might fly apart any second. "Has your mom said anything?"

"She's upstairs getting ready," Zack said, grinning broadly.

Curiosity got the best of Jess and she strutted down the stairs, obviously ignoring her father. "What are we supposed to do tonight?" she asked Zack, her displeasure showing. Mitchell handed her a rented movie that she had been wanting to see. When she didn't say anything, Zack nudged her roughly. "Thanks," she said stiffly.

Upstairs Megan was a mess. She had gotten mascara in her eye and it was bloodshot. Her hair was doing anything but what she wanted it to do. She had changed clothes several times before deciding not to worry about how she looked.

As Megan started down the stairs, Mitchell turned to watch her. The blue silk dress she was wearing was very becoming. The matching heels made her look taller. Her hair fell softly on her shoulders. She had an uneasy look that matched the tension he was feeling.

Jess watched Mitchell as her mother came into view. The look in his eyes gave her a funny feeling and made her angry with her mother.

"You look very handsome," Megan complimented Mitchell as she reached the last step. He smiled at her, speechless.

Jess spoke up. "This is so gross. Mom, I don't know how you could do this!" she said, scowling at them.

Megan overlooked Jess's comment. "What are you two going to do tonight?"

"He brought us a movie," Jess said, nodding in Mitchell's direction.

"That was very thoughtful," she said, flashing Mitchell a nervous smile. "Zack, dinner is in the oven, and Jess can stay up until eleven."

"It smells great," Mitchell commented.

"Would you rather stay here?" Megan said quickly.

"Not tonight. Maybe another time," he said. Then he pointedly checked his watch. "We have reservations for six-thirty. We better get going." He tried once again to warm Jess up a bit. "Hope you enjoy the movie."

She was having none of it. She stood with her arms tightly folded in front of her. He could almost see steam coming out of her ears.

"Have a good time," Zack said, grinning. "And don't rush or anything. We'll be fine." No one missed the glare Jess gave him.

Megan gave Jess a kiss on the cheek, ignoring her bratty behavior. As she reached up to kiss Zack's cheek, he gave her a hug and whispered in her ear, "Thanks, Mom." They gave each other an understanding look.

"See you both tomorrow," Mitchell said. Jess marched out of the room.

"That's my little angel." Megan chuckled.

Mitchell nodded, realizing what she meant. He guided her out the front door and opened the car door for her.

She was about to get in the car, when she noticed a rose on the seat. She was admiring the flower as Mitchell got in. "It's lovely. A competitor?" she asked.

"No way! I have a friend on the inside," he admitted.

She remembered Zack sneaking around that morning. When he came back, he commented that one of the customers had given him a big tip. "Can I assume you're a big tipper?" Megan asked. Mitchell smiled smugly.

They drove to a beautiful old section of town that had been gentrified. Many of the houses had been converted into businesses. The only giveaway that the building was a restaurant was the discreet sign beside the door: Almost Yesterday. Megan had been supplying flowers to the restaurant for the last few months. She knew it was a unique place to have dinner.

Mitchell led her to the front door, and they stepped into the foyer. In the front hall there was an antique desk. While they waited for the hostess, Megan glanced around. The house was decorated with early turn-of-the-century antiques. The golden oak staircase was shining under the glow of lamps and candles.

A parlor off to the left contained several small tables, well spaced and covered with lace tablecloths. The center of each table held a low flower arrangement of spring flowers that Megan had made up that morning.

The hostess appeared and apologized for keeping them waiting. She led them to a small room with a single table. An Irish lace tablecloth and a basket with miniature red roses, wild daisies and baby's breath was placed in the center. Her favorites. Gas logs were burning in the fireplace and candles were placed here and there, giving the room a cozy appearance. The room was decorated with antiques and remembrances of a simpler, more gentle era. It wasn't overdone, just romantic.

After the hostess seated them and left, a gaping silence hung in the air.

"Lovely, isn't it," Megan finally said.

Mitchell glanced about, satisfied. Then his eyes settled on her. "Yes, lovely."

A waiter arrived and began serving them. First, he brought iced tea. Next he brought shrimp cocktails. Megan figured Mitchell had previously ordered everything. Then she noticed all the songs playing in the background were her favorites. She concluded Zack had been in on this too.

Before long a garden salad, baked potato and steak were placed before each of them.

After another long silence, Mitchell asked, "Is everything all right?"

Megan realized that she had been wolfing down her food. "I'm sorry. I missed lunch," she confessed and wiped her mouth. "It's a very nice restaurant."

"I was hoping you'd like it," he admitted.

Megan looked at the stranger across the table from her. This restaurant was totally out of character for the man she knew. So was using her favorite songs. So was the flower arrangement. The rose in the car, that was Mitchell. After that, in times past, he would have taken her to an all-you-can-eat place with pans clanging as background music. To have found a special restaurant like this, with a private room, was unlike him...but she kind of liked it.

Mitchell tried to keep the conversation on safe subjects such as the weather, religion and politics. He steered clear of anything that might end their truce. It had taken most of his courage to arrange the date, knowing it could be a beginning...or an ending.

When Megan realized she'd been set up, she confronted him. "All right, Mitch, what's this all about?"

He sat back and sighed. "You caught me. I asked you out and brought you here with the intention of trying to make a good impression."

"Why did you feel the need to impress me?" she asked curtly.

He stared at her with sadness. "Because I failed you so miserably."

"Don't do this, Mitchell," she said wearily, and turned away.

He restrained himself from reaching out to her. "Will you listen to me, Meg?"

Slowly she turned back. "All right."

Mitchell took his time to make sure he didn't say the wrong thing. "I only want us to get to know one another again."

"This isn't the type of place you go for a get-to-know-one-another dinner," she pointed out, knowing all of this must have been quite expensive. Then she remembered Zack's plea. *You could at least be friends for our sake.* Right behind that she heard Cassie's warning. *Next, he'll be after you.*

"It was the only place I could find with a private dining room for two instead of fifty. I really wanted to take you someplace special," he affirmed.

"How do I know if you're being honest with me?"

"The same way you used to know," he said, his eyes holding hers.

"That's good advice," she mocked. "We know how that turned out." She turned her attention back to her dinner, but she'd lost her appetite.

Waiting for dessert and coffee, Mitchell said, "Dance with me."

Megan loved to dance, too. "No," she said stubbornly.

"Have you forgotten how?" he asked.

"No," she said quietly.

"Then dance with me. I'm not convinced you still know how," he teased, and held out his hand to her. They stared at one another for a moment, then stood up.

Megan closed her eyes and rested her cheek against Mitchell's shoulder. At the moment, his intentions and all the rest of it didn't matter. She was dancing.

He had so much he wanted to say to her. So many things he needed to explain. But he was afraid she might not understand, or that it was too late. So he held her in his arms, and they danced. It was safe for the moment.

The songs went on and on. "Mitchell, this is unfair," Megan whispered.

"No one promised everything would be fair," he whispered back.

Megan began to remember other nights, being held this same way, by this same man. Emotions began to surface, both good and bad. Suddenly she felt overloaded and breathless. She pulled away. "I'm not ready for this."

Mitchell held out her chair for her, but she shook her head. He could tell this was not the time to press. He put a check on the table and guided her outside. He opened the door and helped her into the car. She said nothing.

"I'm sorry," he apologized as he got in the other side.

"For what? A lovely dinner? Dancing with me? Asking me out? Marrying me? What?" she asked exasperatedly, slumping against the door, twirling her engagement ring.

"For pushing you," he admitted, then waited for her to respond. She didn't. He started the car and let it idle. "Are we still on for the movie?" he asked uncertainly.

She glanced over at him, then averted her eyes. "You asked me out for dinner and a movie."

"You don't get out often do you?" he chuckled.

"No, and I haven't been to a movie in ages. Are they still in black and white?"

Mitchell laughed and drove toward the theater. He had picked the picture he thought was the least likely to upset either of them. He bought a box of popcorn and sodas as they entered. They found a seat near the middle of the theater on the end of a row.

The movie started off full force with lots of action. They shared the popcorn as they watched. The action in the middle of the film slowed down considerably. Mitchell reached over and gently took Megan's hand.

She immediately pulled it back, whispering, "I should've known you'd try something!"

"All I want to do is hold your hand!" he whispered back.

They were shushed from behind.

Mitchell leaned closer to her and whispered as quietly as possible, "What's wrong with wanting to hold your hand?"

"You haven't held it for ten years. What's the rush?"

"We haven't been out for ten years."

"That's not *my* fault!" Her whisper rose.

"Would you just give me your hand?" Mitchell insisted.

Several people shushed them again.

"No! Leave me alone." Megan folded her arms firmly in front of her.

Mitchell could be every bit as stubborn as she could. He caught the hand that was closest to him and held it awkwardly.

Megan glared at him fiercely. Then she yanked her hand, using more force than she had intended. Mitchell lost his grip, and her hand flung free. The backlash slugged the man next to her, chopping him across the chest. His box of popcorn flew everywhere.

Megan shot Mitchell a hostile look, then turned to apologize to the man beside her. "Oh, I'm so very sorry," she said, brushing popcorn off the front of his shirt.

The man looked as though he wanted to clobber her. He backed her all the way into her seat and over toward Mitchell. He was a huge man, really mean looking, glowing with anger, and he had popcorn dangling in his hair.

People all around them were shushing them again. Megan glanced at Mitchell. The look on his face finished her off. She threw her hands over her mouth, trying to stifle the hysteria bubbling up inside. It was too late.

She and Mitchell hopped up at the same time and dashed for the back of the theater. He had almost made it, when he heard Megan cackling behind him. He looked back to see her doubled over in the aisle.

He hurried back and dragged her from the theater, before a mob formed and came after them. They collapsed inside the car with tears rolling down their cheeks.

"Zack warned me! He told me you hadn't been out in ages and didn't know how to act," Mitchell kidded.

"Me? You started it!"

"I didn't backhand anyone." They both started laughing all over again. "We better leave before he comes after us," Mitchell said, and drove away.

Megan slumped in her seat, still giggling. They drove around for a while, then Mitchell pulled into the high school parking lot near the athletic field. He sat staring ahead for a while, not saying anything.

"What are we doing here?" Megan asked crisply.

"I don't know. I wanted to be alone somewhere, so we could talk. We met here. It kind of seemed like the right place." He got out of the car and led the way to the bleachers. They climbed to the top and sat down. Memories flooded them both.

Megan patiently waited for him to speak.

Mitchell looked out over the empty field and cleared his throat, but he still sounded like a frog when he spoke. "Meg, I never meant to hurt you. I left to make it easier for you."

She turned her attention from the starry night to him. It was hard to read facial expressions in the moonlight. "I really don't want to talk about this tonight."

"I know. You don't want to talk about it at all. But we have to...sometime."

"Why? Why do we have to talk about it ever again?"

"Because we have nothing to build on as it stands now."

"I wasn't *planning* on building anything."

"Then why did you accept this date with me?"

"For Zack's sake. He wants us to at least be friends."

"What about you? What do you want?" he asked.

She looked up at the sky full of stars. "I want my

children to grow up to be good Christian people. I want
them to go to college and have advantages we never
had. I want them to lead decent lives and make the
most of their time on this earth.''

''I want that for them too. But what about you?'' he
insisted.

''I don't know. I don't think about it much. A day
at a time is all I can manage,'' she said, trying not to
sound pitiful.

They sat in silence for a while. ''Did you ever miss
me, Meg?'' Mitchell asked, his voice full of emotion.

''Of course. It was my fault you left,'' she said, remembering the last visit.

''No, it wasn't. I was looking for an excuse to run
away. All I needed was for you to give me an ulti-
matum,'' he confessed.

She sat still, thinking back. ''I came home from the
hospital thinking you would want to talk. We would
get it all straightened out. Instead, you were gone. Only
a short note to say good-bye. I never thought it would
turn out this way.''

''I knew I was going down,'' he said thoughtfully.
''I didn't want to take you and the kids with me.''

''I believed we could work it out. You gave up. You
gave up on us.'' She fought back the lump growing in
her throat. ''You chose drinking over your family!''

Mitchell closed his eyes and dropped his head. It was
all true. He had to say it and take ownership of his past
mistakes. ''It's true. That was all I cared about at the
time. Nothing else mattered then.''

Megan was shocked to hear him admit it. She looked
over at his slumped silhouette. ''Why wasn't my love
enough?'' she asked, fighting back tears.

''It wasn't you. Please believe that. I didn't know

how to handle problems. When I drank, they didn't matter. If I drank enough, nothing mattered. I got to the point I wanted to stay that way. Then I didn't have to deal with reality."

"I would have done anything to help you."

"It wouldn't have mattered. At the time, I didn't want any help."

"I don't think I'll ever understand."

"It wasn't your fault. You have to know that. It was *my* choice and it was wrong." They sat in silence, each wishing they could understand the other's heart.

Finally, Mitchell stood up and offered Megan his hand. She shook her head. He accepted her refusal. "Want to walk down to the lake?" he asked, subdued.

They walked silently side by side along the path.

"Did you really miss me?" Mitchell asked.

Megan started to speak, then stopped. "Yes," she replied quietly.

They spent a few minutes looking out at the lake reflecting the moonlight, then started back toward the parking lot. They were almost there before she got the courage to ask him, "Did you ever miss *me?*"

Mitchell thought before he answered. He wanted to be honest. "I missed you…when I wasn't drunk. But the more I missed you, the more I drank…so I could forget. It didn't take very long before I was wasted all the time. Then I didn't care about anything. After I bottomed out, I realized what I'd done. I missed you the most then, because I knew what I'd given up. I was so stupid."

They reached the car and Mitch opened the door for her. She slid in, staring straight ahead. He watched her as he continued. "I still miss you. More than you can imagine." He could tell her eyes were filling with tears.

They drove home in silence. There seemed nothing more to say. Mitchell was crushed. He had bared his soul to her and she hadn't even responded. Asking her out on the date had been a mistake.

But Mitchell's words had touched Megan's heart. Why hadn't he told her all this before? She felt so sorry for him. She was afraid that if she said anything, she would start crying, so she didn't speak.

Mitchell pulled in the driveway and turned off the engine. He stared at the old farmhouse. It reminded him of Megan's parents' home. "Remember the night I brought you home and we were having a big fight? We got out of the car and stood in the front yard yelling at one another."

Megan suddenly smiled at the memory. "We must have gone on forever."

"Yeah, well, until your dad threw that shoe out the window." He chuckled.

"It hit me right in the head," she said, rubbing the place. "I had a big bump, remember?"

"You wouldn't let me forget. You showed it to me fifty times a day and told me it was all my fault," Mitchell said, smiling slightly.

"It was! You yelled so loud you woke Daddy up," she pointed out, grinning. "Besides, I wanted you to suffer with me."

"How about the time your mother came out on the porch to bring us some ice cream and caught us kissing?" he continued.

She laughed. "You were so embarrassed. Your face turned red and melted the ice cream. And what about the day we skipped school to go to the lake swimming and your mother was there waiting for us? I wanted to disappear. Then you told her it was *my* idea!"

"It *was* your idea. Besides, I wanted to take some of the heat off me," Mitchell said, watching her.

"Your mother called my parents and told them. They hit the ceiling. They told me I was never to see you again—you were trouble," she admitted.

"I never knew that." He frowned.

"I never told you. I came and talked to your mother and asked her to talk to my parents. I don't know what she said, but they had a chat with me. They told me I could still see you, but there better not be any more trouble. God bless your mother. I don't know what I'd do without her."

Suddenly the mood had changed and they were on old familiar ground. Mitchell gazed over at Megan. "You were always so much fun. I never knew what you'd do next...kind of like tonight."

"Mitchell, you know that was your fault. That poor man!" She looked over at him. He was so familiar, yet he was different. And she didn't want to admit that tonight was the most fun she'd had in a long time.

"All I wanted was for you to hold my hand," he said quietly, and held one hand open before her. She placed her hand in his, and he gripped it firmly. Mitchell leaned toward her and the porch light came on. "Who has timing like your father?"

"Probably the child who should be in bed by now," Megan told him. She carried her rose as they walked to the house.

At the door, in the porch light, Mitchell suddenly felt self-conscious. He looked around and complimented her on the house, the flowers, the yard. At last he turned his attention back to her. She was equally ill at ease.

"Was it so bad?" he finally asked.

She rolled her eyes, smiling. "Yes...and no."

"Would you consider going out with me again?" he asked timidly. Then he realized how much like high school that sounded.

She smiled at his unsophisticated approach. Their eyes held for a few seconds, each with an uncertain reflection. Then Megan giggled. "You have my number. Call me."

Mitchell laughed heartily. With all the charm he could muster, he asked, "Do I get a good-night kiss?"

Megan considered his request for a few seconds. Then the thought hit her that they might be under surveillance. "Not on the first date!"

"Your daddy's not in there to throw shoes at us," he said, moving closer.

"I know, it's worse. Jess is in there," she said smoothly and started to escape.

Mitchell stopped her gently. "I'll risk it." Unhurriedly he took her in his arms. She looked at him wide-eyed. Her eyes closed as he moved toward her. He kissed her tenderly, but firmly. Then he waited to see how she would react.

Megan backed away slowly. "It was a special evening. Thank you," she said, giving him an uncertain smile before escaping into the house.

Mitch sighed as he walked to the car. She was all he remembered and more.

As soon as his mother came in the door, Zack was on his feet. "So, how did it go?" he asked breathlessly.

"Oh, it was an emotional roller coaster," she said, crinkling up her face.

"Is that good or bad?" he asked, fishing for information.

"Neither," she said.

"Are you going out with him again?"

"Maybe," she said, keeping her answer noncommittal. She put the inquisition to an end by heading up the stairs.

Zack quickly thought of another question. "How was the movie?"

Megan burst out laughing. "Really funny!"

"I thought you were going to the thriller?" he said, trying to keep her talking.

"We did," Megan grinned, dashing up the rest of the steps.

Zack frowned, realizing he was missing something.

Chapter Five

After "the date," Mitchell was often in and out of the house picking up the children, but he gave Megan a little space. She wasn't exactly cold, just indifferent. When he invited her to join them, she always had a reasonable excuse not to come along.

Mitchell noticed one of the gutters and a couple of shutters on her house were coming loose after a storm. One afternoon he and Zack decided to repair them.

Megan came home from work as they were finishing up. She barely spoke and hurried into the house.

When Mitchell came in to wash his hands, Megan was at the sink. She was staring out the window, remembering a phone conversation she had had earlier with Cass.

"Megan, I heard you're still letting that man see the children. What on earth is wrong with you?" Cass had started.

"Cass, it's my problem, not yours," she said, tired of her sister's interference.

"You know what I mean. He'll bring trouble. Get

him out of your life or you're going to be sorry! I'm concerned about you, can't you see that?'' Cass hung up quickly before her sister could respond.

When she came home and found Mitchell working on her house, it made her angry because he hadn't asked. Now here he was coming in the house like he owned the place. Megan moved out of his way and spoke sharply. ''I was going to hire someone to repair my house.''

Mitchell turned to face her as he dried his hands. ''I did it because I wanted to.''

''Thank you. What do I owe you?'' she asked curtly.

''Nothing. Absolutely nothing at all,'' he answered, perturbed.

''It's my house. I can take care of it.''

''I'm sure you can. I didn't intended to step on your turf. I guess I overstepped my bounds. I'm sorry,'' he explained, feeling a little put out.

''Stay for dinner if you like, as repayment,'' she said stiffly.

Mitchell recognized that this was not a genuine invitation, only an obligation to repay a debt. ''No, thank you,'' he said and walked out.

Megan watched him drive away, feeling self-righteous.

Sleep didn't come easily to Megan that night. Her conscience was bothering her. She would have been grateful for the help, if the repairman had been anyone other than her estranged husband.

Understanding her own reasons didn't solve the problem or soothe her conscience. It crossed her grain to treat anyone unkindly, even Mitchell.

She tried to pray. ''Heavenly Father, I'm sorry for the way I treated Mitchell. I know I should be grateful, but…'' Her prayers seemed to bounce off the ceiling and come right back to her. She tossed and turned most of the night.

Days passed without Mitchell coming in with the kids. On Monday he took them shopping after school. It was a beautiful spring day and Megan decided to cook out. She had everything almost ready when Mitchell's car pulled in the driveway.

Zack saw the grill, leaped out of the car and dashed over to his mother. "Mom, why don't you invite Dad to stay for dinner?"

She started to make an excuse. "I'm not sure he—"

"Please, Mom, go ask him. Do it for me," Zack begged.

She knew she needed to try to end this rift with Mitchell if she wanted peace with God. She walked toward his car. Jess got out with her arms loaded and slammed the door.

Mitchell started backing out of the driveway.

Megan started running after the car, waving and shouting. When Mitchell saw her, he ground to a halt and rolled the window down. "I'm cooking out to-night. I thought maybe you'd like to stay for dinner," she said breathlessly.

Mitchell knew this wasn't her idea. He was tired of this second-rate treatment. "No, thanks," he said, backing up again.

Megan felt she had done her part by offering the olive branch—until she noticed Zack and Jess watching. She spun around and called, "Wait!"

Once again Mitchell stopped, not sure why he kept putting himself in this position. Megan stooped down by the window.

"I'm sorry for the way I behaved the other night. I have a lot of excuses, but none of them are very good. I want to apologize for my uncalled-for behavior. I hope you can forgive me," she said sincerely. He glanced at her skeptically. "I didn't plan to cook out until the last minute. I know it's late to ask, but if you don't have any plans, we'd like you to stay."

She noticed smoke rising from the grill. "Dinner's about to burn. It's up to you," she said, dashing to save dinner.

Mitchell considered the offer. Was she crazy? Of course he wanted to stay! He'd just wanted her to make a move. The kids were still watching as he got out of the car. Zack grinned. Jess frowned and kicked the dirt.

"Do you mind if I say the blessing?" Mitchell asked, offering his hands to his children as they sat at the picnic table. Zack readily took one of his hands. Megan had to nudge Jess to get her to take the other one.

"Lord, thank you for bringing us together to share this meal. We ask that you bless the food and each of us. In Jesus' name, amen," he prayed.

Zack managed to fill the gaping holes in the conversation during dinner. When they finished eating, he said, "Mom, Jess and I will clean up the dishes." Jess looked at him as though he was out of his mind.

"Would you like to go for a walk?" Mitchell suggested, noticing Megan looked uneasy. She nodded, glad to be doing something. He loosened his tie as they walked down by the river. They stopped on the foot-bridge, watching the river run its course.

"Up to a little climb?" Megan asked, figuring he would point out that he wasn't dressed for the occasion.

"Where?" he asked curiously.

"To my hill," she said, pointing to the path.

"Sure," Mitchell agreed. Zack had told him that this was his mother's favorite spot. He felt privileged to be asked to see it.

Megan took the lead and scrambled up the trail, wondering how long it would be before he quit.

Mitchell knew the terrain was tearing up his dress shoes and snagging his slacks, but he wasn't about to turn back.

At the top Megan looked out over her farm. Mitchell stood beside her and did the same. "Nice view," he remarked.

Megan turned without comment and continued to the old rock. Climbing onto it, she waited to see what he would do.

"Come here often?" Mitchell asked as he seated himself on the same rock.

"Depends on how things are going. Seems like I spend more time up here when things aren't going too well," she admitted.

"Is this your getaway?"

"I guess it is. I come here alone to be quiet and listen to God."

"Everyone needs a place like that," he said, understanding.

"Do you have a special place?" she asked.

"Not a permanent one. I camped out west once and climbed a butte. I just sat there looking out over the desert. It was the most spiritual place I've ever been. The whispering wind was the only thing breaking the silence," he said, seeming far away.

"Sounds special," Megan remarked, wondering about the places he'd been.

"It is. I'd like to go back there someday. I know you'd like it."

The sun was nearing the horizon when Megan slid off the rock. "We better start back before it gets dark."

They picked their steps going down the hill, pausing for one last look at the setting sun. As they walked back, Mitchell had something to say, and he decided he might as well say it now. "Meg, I feel like I'm on trial with you. And no matter what I do, somehow it's going to be wrong."

"Then stop overdoing it," she grumbled.

"What have I done wrong now?"

"Nothing. I just feel as though you watch every move I make. You read something into everything I do. It's like being under a microscope."

"I feel as though if I step over that imaginary line you draw, you'll tell me to get lost. You just want me to be daddy to the kids and pretend you don't exist. It's hard to act as if I don't care, when I spend most of my time thinking about you. Can't we be a little more considerate of each other's feelings?" he asked.

Megan stared off into the distance. It was true. She wanted to keep him at a distance, a far off, safe distance. She felt so vulnerable around him. It scared her. "I can't help how I feel," she said quietly.

"Am I supposed to give up? I can't do that. Tell me what you want me to do—and I'll do it," he said, feeling discouraged.

"Be yourself. If I don't like it, you'll know," she said sternly.

"You've gotten tough."

She looked him straight in the eye. "I had to get tough to survive." He felt wounded by her words, yet he knew he deserved them.

As they came in the kitchen, Jess was at the table eating a bowl of ice cream. She looked at them with disgust, put her bowl in the sink, and stomped off.

"What's with her?" Mitchell asked, dumbfounded.

"You showed up and turned her world upside down! Suddenly she's forced to go out with a strange man named 'Daddy.'"

"I hadn't thought of it that way. I'd be angry too, if I were in her position."

"You scare her," Megan added as they sat across the table from one another.

"The same way I scare you?" he asked.

She nodded reluctantly.

He reached across the table and touched the diamond on her engagement ring. He gently moved it from side to side. "Why did you tell me that about Jess?"

"It's hard being a kid. But sometimes it is even harder being a parent. She needs a father, whether she likes it or not."

Mitchell gently covered her hand with his. Then he looked at her to see if he needed to duck. Unexpectedly, Megan smiled at him. He wished he could take her in his arms and hold her tight.

As though she'd read his thoughts, she pulled her hand away.

"Thanks for dinner and the walk. I guess I better get out of your way," he said, not wanting to wear out his welcome.

"You're not leaving?" Zack asked, coming in the kitchen with his books in his arms. "I need some help with math, and Mom is awful."

"Don't go on my account. I'm going to watch a movie," Megan said, leaving the kitchen. Shortly afterward, she heard the two of them laughing. It was a good sound.

Before long Jess came downstairs and curled up beside her mother on the sofa. "I don't like all that noise they're making," she complained.

"I'm sorry they're bothering you," Megan said, snuggling her closer.

Jess grumbled a little while longer, then fell asleep curled against her mother.

Mitchell came to say good-night before he left, and found Jess protectively wrapped in her mother's arms. Both were asleep. He took advantage of the situation and kissed Jess on the cheek. He turned to do the same to Megan and found her wide-eyed.

"I'm going. See ya soon," he whispered. Deciding to risk it, he kissed her on the cheek, then rushed out.

Megan was smiling to herself as her eyes drifted closed.

A couple of nights later Mitchell showed up at dinnertime with a pizza. He found Megan at the kitchen table doing book work. "I thought I'd drop this by to thank you for dinner the other night," he said, handing her the box and starting for the door.

"Why don't you stay?" Megan asked.

That had been his original intention, but now he was feeling a bit guilty.

"Wasn't that what you had in mind?" Megan asked, letting him know she saw right through him.

"If you insist," he said, satisfied.

"Would you make a salad, while I get my mess out of the way?" she asked.

Mitchell rolled up his sleeves and began looking

through the refrigerator for ingredients. When the kids came in for dinner, he got the usual reaction from each.

After dinner Megan went back to her book work. Zack talked his father into playing Scrabble. Jess followed them to the family room, then pretended she was reading. As father and son played, Jess felt left out, but refused to join them. At bedtime she went over to Mitchell. "I have to go to bed now."

"'Night Jess," he said, longing to hug her.

"'Night," she said, looking glum.

Knowing his mother was still working in the kitchen, Zack said good-night to his father and raced Jess up the stairs.

"Do you ever stop working?" Mitchell asked when he came in the kitchen.

Megan leaned back in the chair, yawning. "I'm almost finished."

The radio was playing an old familiar song about the best of romances deserving second chances. Mitchell pulled Megan out of the chair and into his arms, dancing her around the kitchen. "Go out with me Saturday night."

"No!" she said, trying to pull away.

The song was almost over. Mitchell dipped her back and held her there. "Say yes," he insisted, smiling.

"Or what? You'll break my back?" She giggled.

He pulled her back up. Still holding her, he waited for an answer.

"I don't know," she said, stalling.

She had that guarded look he had come to know so well. "I know I was a rotten no-good drunk," he said with his throat tightening. She tried to turn away, but he caught her face in his hands. "I was also a lousy husband and father. But I'm changing. God knows I am. I love you, Megan. You have to believe that,'' he said.

A tear slid down her cheek as their eyes held in a long, engaging stare.

"Say you'll go out with me Saturday night," he pressed. She searched his face, looking for answers. "Give us a chance, Meg. That's all I'm asking." He nudged her a little as a tear slid down his own cheek.

Slowly she nodded, as Mitchell wiped her tears and lightly kissed her cheek. "I'm leaving before you change your mind," he said, smiling nervously.

Megan's heart raced as he left. Had she lost her mind?

The next night her mother called. "Megan, your father and I are worried about you," she said.

"What if…" she began uncertainly.

"You think he's changed," her mother said with a sigh.

"I'm not sure. How do you know something like that?"

"I guess by actions. Are you seeing him?"

"Officially once," Megan admitted and heard her mother groan. "Mom, he was a gentleman. He planned dinner at this special little restaurant. He ordered my favorite flowers and food and music. It was so nice. The old Mitchell would never have done that. Then we went to the movies. Well, that's a story in itself," she said, laughing at the memory. "Later, we drove to the high school and sat on the bleachers talking. It was really hard for both of us. But you know Mom, I really had a good time. I've never stopped missing Mitch."

"And later?" her mother asked gingerly.

"He brought me home. We said good-night at the door."

"Did he kiss you?" her mother pried.

"Mother!"

"Well, I was just curious." She laughed.

"The answer is yes. A sweet little kiss. I'm confused, Mom."

"I've tried to put myself in your position. It's hard. What are you going to do?"

"I don't know."

"If everything fell apart between your father and myself, I think I'd still love him. No one could take his place in my heart," she confessed.

"Then you know how I feel?" Megan said, needing someone to understand.

"Kind of." Her mother's voice was full of empathy. "But you can't go by feelings alone. They aren't always reliable."

"I know. He wants me to go out again," she said.

"I wish I could tell you the right thing to do, but we each have to decide our own course. I'll pray for you—both of you," her mother said.

"Thanks, Mom. I love you," Megan said, and hung up.

Mitchell was planning to take the children to a mud bog on Friday night. "Would you like to tag along?" he asked Megan.

"I don't have any idea what a mud bog is, but I'm sure I don't want to find out. I have to wash my hair or brush my teeth or something equally important. I couldn't possibly change my plans," she kidded him.

Mitchell laughed heartily. "In that case, I'll see you Saturday night!"

On Friday night, Zack and Jess were ready half an hour early. Mitchell was late, which was rare. When the phone rang, Zack dove for it. He listened and hung up. "That was Dad. Something came up at the last minute. He'll be here as soon as possible."

Uneasiness began to stir in Megan. She went to the kitchen and puttered around.

Two hours later, they were all on edge and trying to stay out of each other's way.

The phone finally rang again. Zack answered, listened for a minute, then handed it to his mother. "It's Doc," he said, disappointed.

Megan took the phone. "Hi, Doc."

"I need for you to come to the hospital right away," he said, sounding strange.

"Why? What's wrong?"

"Mitchell's been hurt."

"So that's why he's late," she scoffed.

"Ruth and the kids should come too," he said solemnly.

"He's okay, isn't he?" When Doc hesitated, fear suddenly surged through her.

"Just get here soon."

"I'll be right there," she said, hanging up.

She turned to the children and started explaining. "Your father's been hurt. Zack, you and Jess go pick up Gran and meet me at the hospital." Zack herded Jess out the door, while Megan called Ruth.

Doc met her at the emergency room door.

"How's Mitch?" she asked immediately.

"He's been badly beaten. He's in surgery now with a head injury."

"Beaten!" she said, astounded.

"He also has some broken bones and internal damage. He's in pretty bad shape," Doc told her. She sank into a nearby chair.

"Somebody beat Mitchell nearly to death. Why? It doesn't make any sense." Suddenly it did. "Drugs were involved, weren't they?" she said sharply, looking at him.

"All I heard was it had something to do with a kid and a drug dealer. I don't know how Mitchell got involved. Don't jump to any conclusions," he warned, but he could see that she already had.

At that moment, Ruth and the children came rushing down the hall. Megan felt numb. How could she have been so wrong again?

When Ruth understood the gravity of the situation, she began to cry. "I just got him back. Please, dear Lord, don't take him from me."

Megan gave Ruth the chair and began wandering down the hall. She leaned against the tile wall. "Why Mitchell?" she whispered.

Doc went to her and put his arm around her. "Listen, Megan, I don't know what really happened and neither do you. Mitchell needs you right now. So put your feelings aside and be there for him. Understand."

"Why does he need me here?" she asked. Then it all sank in. He was afraid that Mitchell was going to die....

Doc took them to the intensive care unit and got the latest report. Mitchell had made it through surgery.

Later Doc took Megan in to see him. She glanced at the body flowing with monitors and tubes. Finally she looked at his face and gaped in shock.

"He's alive," Doc reminded her.

She moved a little closer, gently brushing his cheek

with her finger. "Mitch, it's Megan. Talk to me," she said in a low, soothing voice, more calmly than she felt.

Doc watched the monitors as she spoke. "Keep talking to him."

"You're going to be fine. Your mother and Zack and Jess are waiting to see you. Why don't you open your eyes now?" she asked. She got no response at all.

"Keep going," Doc encouraged, then went to join the others. "You'll have to go in one at a time and you can only stay for a few minutes. He's not conscious, so he won't know you. But I feel sure he'll know you're there."

Ruth stood up. "I'd like to go first." Doc led her to the ICU.

Megan started to move away, but Doc caught her hand. "Please don't leave him," he whispered, his eyes begging her. He pulled a chair over by the bed for her.

Ruth gently kissed Mitchell's bandaged head. "I love you, son. Don't give up," she told him and returned to the waiting room.

Doc brought Jess in next. He only let her stay for a few seconds.

When Zack came in, he leaned over his father and whispered, "Don't give up! I need you...I love you, Dad."

Doc seated Megan in the chair before he took Zack out.

"Is my dad going to die?" Zack asked the doctor. He didn't know much about medical terms, but he could tell his father was in bad shape.

"Not if we can help it," Doc replied.

"Your dad's a tough guy. He's not going to give up without a fight. But we all need to be fighting. Doc, where's the hospital chapel?'' Ruth asked getting to her feet.

It had been a while since Doc had been to the chapel. He'd lost faith in praying when his wife died. His faith was in medicine, but the medical profession had done all it could do for Mitchell. He doubted the man would make it through the night.

Ruth sat in a pew with Zack and Jess. She bowed her head and began to pray aloud scriptures from the Bible, God's promises to His children. She wasn't going to give up her son without all the fight that was within her.

Zack didn't know the Bible the way his grandmother did, but he too began to pray for his father to be healed. He'd lost him once, he wasn't willing to again.

Jess listened. Then she prayed silently.

Doc stood in the back of the chapel, listening. He wished he could believe it would make a difference, but he couldn't. He slipped out quietly.

Megan sat looking at Mitchell. Each time a doctor checked him, she asked if there was any improvement. They shook their heads and looked grim.

Doc came in a while later and noticed she was looking weary. ''Zack wants to see his father. Why don't you get a cup of coffee?'' he suggested.

Megan hugged Zack as they changed places. In the waiting room she found Jess asleep in Ruth's lap. Ruth's eyes were closed. Megan knew she was praying.

Starting for the coffee shop, she detoured to the chapel. Sitting near the empty cross, she began crying. *I don't want him to die. I hate to admit it, but I'd miss him.*

Suddenly she realized that sitting there crying wasn't

doing Mitchell any good at all. She dried her eyes, picked up a Bible and opened it, trying to concentrate.

Dropping to her knees she prayed, "Lord, what must I do? I know You're the only one who can help Mitchell. The doctors have given up. I can see it in their eyes. Lord, You can help him. I know You can. It couldn't be Your plan to bring him home, just to let him die. Let this be Your will. Whatever You want me to do, I'll do it. In Jesus' name, I pray. Amen."

Megan let her head fall to her chest in submission to God. As she did, the Bible began to slip off her lap. She grabbed for it and noticed the words in red letters. They seemed to jump out at her.

She read the passage from the book of Mark aloud. "Have faith in God. For assuredly, I say to you, whoever says to this mountain, 'Be removed and cast into the sea,' and does not doubt in his heart, but believes that those things he says will be done, he will have whatever he says. Therefore I say to you, whatever things you ask when you pray, believe that you receive them, and you will have them."

Megan looked up and prayed. "God, I know there's nothing I can do for Mitchell. But You can. Lord, I'm asking you to heal Mitchell's broken body. Make him whole and well again. His children and mother need him. You say in Your word not to doubt. Everything looks bad. But I've been in other places in my life where it looked impossible. You've always been faithful. Lord, I won't look at the circumstances. I'll only believe in You. Your will be done in Jesus' name. Amen."

Megan knelt in silence, waiting. She knew she should return to ICU soon. Mitchell needed a reason to live.

As she came back in the cubicle, she touched Zack's shoulder. He seemed to be lost in thought. He turned to face his mother and his face crumpled. "Don't say it," she said calmly. "Go sit with Gran."

Megan sat down beside Mitchell. He looked worse than before. "I'm going to believe You, Lord. I trust You. Only You," she confessed out loud.

She touched Mitchell's cheek. "Come on, Mitch, wake up," she said softly. "You've already missed so much." She started telling him all about the things he'd missed over the years.

The doctors came by, but she refused to question them. Her eyes told her he was getting close to death, but her heart told her not to give up.

Even Megan's mind told her, "It's almost over, give up. Sometimes the answer to prayer is 'no.' He's dying, let him go in peace." Her heart refused to accept that. "What must I do, Lord?" she whispered.

The answer came. *Tell him what's in your heart.*

Megan knew God wanted her to stand in faith for Mitchell's life. She knew Jesus could heal him. Mitchell looked dreadful. 2 Corinthians 5:7 came to mind. "For we walk by faith, not by sight." She knew that she had to turn her thoughts off and concentrate on God's ability.

She took a deep breath and boldly began to speak. "Mitchell, I believe God is faithful and more than able to take care of you. I'm looking at God, not the circumstances." It was a tall order, but she bowed her head. "I said I would do whatever You asked, Lord. Help me," she prayed.

She leaned near him. "Mitchell, I want you to wake up and talk to me. Your job here isn't finished. You have two children who need you to teach them all about life.'' Her words felt flat and lifeless. She felt she wasn't doing him any good.

She knew she had to tell him the secrets of her heart that no one else knew. She started again. ''Mitch, I know we've had our share of problems, but you know what? We can work them out. I need for you to help me raise Zack and Jess. It's really hard alone. Since you came back, I've felt that if I needed a little moral support with the kids, you'd be there. I know you'd help me, even though I've never asked. You can't imagine how mad I am with you. Sometimes I'd like to just shake you. I want you to make me understand why you left me. I really don't want to be alone. I see the kids going away from me, to lives of their own and I'm afraid I'll be old and bitter and alone.'' She wiped at the tears that began to fall.

''When we went out, you asked me if I'd missed you. I couldn't tell you, because I was afraid I'd cry in front of you.'' She put her lips lightly against his cheek. ''Of course I missed you,'' she whispered. ''You really shocked me by coming back. I'd figured I'd seen the last of Mitchell Whitney.'' She laughed lightly as tears streamed down her face.

She laid her head on the pillow beside him. ''It's not your time to die, Mitchell. God isn't finished with you yet. You haven't fulfilled your purpose here. We still have a lot of things we need to talk about. You need to open your eyes. Stick around and help me. You'll break my heart all over again if you leave me…because I still love you.'' She kissed his cheek.

''You know we promised God we'd be together until death. I'm not ready for the end yet. Try, Mitch. You're a fighter, don't give up. I need you…''

Zack and Doc entered the room, stopping when they

saw that Megan's eyes were closed as she whispered in Mitchell's ear.

Zack lightly touched his mother's shoulder. Her eyes flew open and she saw that Mitchell was awake. "Oh! Thank you, God! Thank you," she cried.

The next thing Megan knew she was out in the hall and a flood of doctors had taken over. Ruth heard the commotion and came to see what was going on. "Dad woke up!" Zack hooted.

"Praise the Lord!" Ruth threw her arms up in the air.

"Where's Jess?" Megan asked.

"She's asleep in the waiting room," Ruth answered.

Megan looked at her mother-in-law with tears in her eyes. "I'll be back in a few minutes." She found herself in the chapel again, staring up at the empty cross. "Thank you, Lord."

When Megan returned, Doc was trying to convince Ruth and Zack that they shouldn't get overly confident. "Mitchell's a long way from well. He might have brain damage or be otherwise permanently disabled," he warned.

Megan heard the end of the conversation. "He'll be fine," she said unwaveringly.

"I hope so. Why don't you all go home and get some rest?" he suggested.

"That's a good idea," she said confidently. "I know he'll continue healing."

Doc was about to give her a warning about faith, when Megan sat down beside Jess. He watched her gently patting her sleeping daughter, like she used to do when Jess was a tiny baby. He decided not to say anything.

* * *

Back at the farmhouse, Ruth looked her daughter-in-law in the eye. "Thank you."

Megan felt awkward. "I didn't do anything but talk to him. Thank God. Now go get some rest, please. You look so tired."

Megan dropped in one of the kitchen chairs. She was wired and exhausted at the same time. She glanced at the clock. The shop was due to open in an hour. She picked herself up and went to take a shower.

After opening, Megan brought Ted up-to-date on what had happened.

"If I can help, just say so," Ted said.

After work Megan drove to the hospital. She went by the business office first to take care of the insurance. To her surprise, it had already been handled.

Next, she found Mitchell had been moved from ICU to a private room. Carrying a flower arrangement, she entered the room. Mitchell's eyes moved to her as soon as the door opened. She walked over to the bed, smiling warmly. "Hi."

He looked awful. He tried to speak, but she couldn't understand him. "Feeling a little rough, huh," she said, glancing around the room. Ruth was in the chair by the window with Jess wedged in beside her. Zack was leaning against the wall. She put the flowers by the window. "Did any of you get any rest?" They all nodded.

Megan turned back to Mitchell, and he watched as she took inventory of his injuries. His left arm was in a cast up past his elbow. His ribs were taped. He was stitched over his eye, under his lip, and several places on his body. His head was wrapped like a mummy, and one foot was bandaged. His face was swollen worse than it had been the night before. All in all, he looked pitiful.

"Zack, why don't we let your mom take over?" Ruth suggested, knowing her son wanted some time alone with Megan. The three of them told Mitchell good-night.

Alone with the patient, Megan sat in the chair beside the bed and smiled at him wickedly. "This was a little extreme to get out of taking me dancing," she teased.

He muttered something that sounded like, "I'd rather be dancing."

She sighed heavily. "I want to know the truth about what happened."

He said something. It sounded like, "wrong place, right time."

She shook her head in disgust. "You nearly died. Was it worth it?"

He thought for a few seconds, then nodded.

"Ah, Mitch. I thought you'd changed. I thought this kind of mess was behind you. How could you?" she said, both angry and hurt at what she thought he'd done.

Mitchell's eyes welled up and he closed them.

Megan knew she had upset him. She could have kicked herself. She found a tissue and dabbed the tears from his eyes. "I'm sorry. I shouldn't have said anything. I don't know what really happened. Forgive me," she apologized, taking his hand in hers.

Mitchell slowly opened his eyes. She saw he was in a great deal of pain. "Can I do anything for you?" she asked sincerely.

He tried to say something, but she couldn't understand him. He tried again. This time she understood. "Believe in me."

Megan stared at him. He wanted her to do something tough. "I'll try."

The rest of the evening, she made him as comfortable as possible. She told him funny little things the children did, trying to cheer him up. Later, she could tell he was getting tired. "I should go and let you get some rest."

"No!" he pleaded. Megan covered him and held his hand until she was sure he was asleep. Then she slipped quietly out of the room. As she drove home, his words kept echoing in her head. *Believe in me!*

Chapter Six

Slowly, Mitchell began to heal. Ruth spent her days at the hospital with her son. Zack and Jess took over after school. In the evenings, Megan would slip in at the end of visiting hours. All their lives now revolved around the hospital room.

One evening Doc was waiting for Megan when she came out of Mitchell's room. "You're just the person I wanted to see. How's Mitch?" he asked cheerfully.

She shrugged. "He seems kind of depressed to me."

"I'm sure just seeing you made him feel better," he said, smiling. Then he took her by the arm and led her down the hall. "Could I talk to you for a few minutes?"

"Is something wrong?" she asked, concerned.

He shook his head and took her into an empty office. "I have something to ask you. This will be just between us. Whatever you decide, no one else will ever know we had this conversation."

"What going on?" she asked suspiciously.

Doc rubbed his chin thoughtfully. "You know the

high cost of medical care is forcing us to do things that we don't like, but we have to conform.'' Megan nodded. ''The insurance company is pushing us to release Mitchell. We've basically done all that we can do. Now he needs time to rest and mend. I have several options. Will you listen to them?''

Megan leaned back and sighed. She could tell by the way he was acting that she was not going to like the gist of this conversation. ''Go ahead.''

''Number one, Mitchell could go to a nursing home. Of course, they are very expensive and he may not do well in one. Number two, Ruth could take him home, but we both know she isn't capable of caring for him all by herself. Nurses could be hired, but that's expensive too,'' he said, eyeing her seriously.

''Or number three, he could go to your house and all of you could pitch in and take care of him the way you're doing here,'' he said in the same even tone.

Megan closed her eyes and rubbed her temples.

''Now, Megan, I know this is not the ideal situation, but where else does he have to go?'' Doc asked.

''Have you talked to him about this?'' she asked shortly.

''No! As I said, this is my idea. Neither Mitchell nor Ruth knows anything about it. I just thought that if I were in his position, I would want to be with my family. Will you at least think about it?''

''When do you have to know?'' Megan asked.

''Soon. The hospital is being pushed to release him,'' he repeated.

''I need to think about it. Do you know what happened the night he was beaten up?'' she asked.

''I wasn't there when he came in. I know the police

have been in to question him. They didn't seem to have
a problem with him,'' he said.

"I have two children to think about, you know,''
she snapped.

"I understand that. If I thought there was a problem,
I would never ask you to do this,'' he assured her.

"Why, Doc? Haven't I had enough grief from
Mitch? Do I need any more?'' she asked, dropping her
head, already feeling the pressure closing in on her.

"I know this is asking a lot. But I have to think
about what's best for my patient—and that's you. We
would have lost him if it hadn't been for you. If you
can't do it, just tell me. Other arrangements can be
made,'' he said, walking her to the parking lot.

Megan drove home with Doc's request rolling
around in her head. She didn't want to do this. She
already knew what Zack would say. He would want to
move Mitch in right away. Jess, on the other hand,
would have the opposite reaction. That left it in her lap
again.

The next day Megan jumped every time the phone
rang, thinking it would be the hospital telling her it
was time for Mitchell to get out.

Ted noticed she was distracted. "You okay?'' he
asked casually.

"Actually, I'm really tired,'' she admitted.

Ted offered to take care of things, and she thanked
him and left.

She drove down the dirt road toward the river and
climbed to her usual spot on the hill. She started weigh-
ing the options. Ruth's house. She would take him
home without a second thought. She wouldn't want to
hire any help, thinking she could do it herself. In the

process she'd overdo it and wear herself out. Then Megan would have to take care of *both* of them.

Next, she considered a nursing home. She knew he would get proper care, but the thought of it disheartened her. She had no idea what Mitchell's financial status might be. Neither she nor Ruth could afford round-the-clock nurses.

Unfortunately, that left *her* house. She contemplated the children looking after their father. What would she do if the police came after him? There would be tons of extra work. She would never have a minute to herself. Jess would be livid! Zack would help, so would Ruth. She tried to weigh every possible problem that could arise.

Eventually, Mitchell crossed her thoughts. In all her grand plans, she'd never counted on anything like this. Her head told her not to get involved. It said, *Let him go to a nursing home or let Ruth take him in. It's not your problem. He deserted you. Let him figure this out for himself.*

Her heart told her to have compassion. She thought of the story of the Good Samaritan. Would she be the one that saw someone in need and crossed to the other side of the road and passed by? Or would she be the one who stopped and helped?

She remembered back to every hard decision she had ever made. She had always called on God for help. This was no time to go it alone.

"What should I do, Lord?" she asked aloud. She sighed. She knew His answer. She just wasn't sure she liked it. "Why, God? Why me?" she cried out. "What have I done to deserve this?" Then she remembered the night at the hospital. She had promised God she would do whatever He asked her to do.

"I've been hoping You would come up with someone else to take care of this situation," she admitted to
God aloud. "I guess not, huh? You want me to do it.
How come I have to take care of him, when he hasn't
been there for me? It's not fair!" Then she was reminded of her words to Mitchell during their wedding,
I promise...until death do us part.

She recalled when Mitchell woke in the hospital,
how grateful she had been. Later, he asked her to believe in him. The Thurlows had believed in her. They
had given her a chance when no one else would. That
was what God and Mitchell were asking her to do—at
least give him a chance.

She stared at the two rings she always wore. She had
made promises to God and to Mitch on their wedding
day. She still believed those promises. Megan lifted her
face to the heavens. "All right, I'll do it Your way,"
she cried out.

That same night she went to the hospital as usual.
Doc was with Mitchell when she came in the room.
She wore a much brighter smile than she felt. "Well,
Doc, how's the patient doing?"

"Making progress like a snail," he grumbled.

She winked at Doc, then stood close to Mitchell. He
had the same apologetic, hurt expression as before on
his face. He looked like a wounded puppy who had
been kicked around, but was still hoping for attention
and acceptance.

"Maybe I could get him moving faster if he came
home!" she said smoothly.

"Why didn't I think of that?" Doc grinned at her.
"That's a great idea. How about tomorrow?"

So soon? She'd been hoping she would have a little

time to prepare Zack and Jess and herself. She couldn't let Mitch see her dismay. She quickly went over to a new flower arrangement beside the bed and pretended to admire it.

"I can't go to your house," he moaned.

Megan glanced over her shoulder at him. "Of course you can. It's settled."

Mitchell looked to Doc for help. "Go home with Megan, get yourself back together. Everything will work out," he advised.

"Not like this," Mitchell pleaded.

Megan swallowed her pride and sat down beside his bed. "Mitch, I want you to come home until you get back on your feet. Everything else can wait until later. Right now, your getting better is all that matters."

She sounded very convincing, but he noticed she was twirling her engagement ring. He wanted to believe that she wanted him to come home, but he knew it wasn't true. She was going through the motions, but her heart really wasn't in it. He wanted to go home as her husband—not as an invalid. "No!" he said.

"My mind is made up. Are you up to changing it?" Megan teased, knowing he was feeling bullied. He looked at her pitifully. He wasn't up to anything—and she knew it.

Megan prepared to leave. "I need to get home and get things ready for tomorrow," she said cheerfully. "I'll pick you up in the morning." Mitchell still had a don't-go look on his face. "I'll see you first thing tomorrow," she said, hurrying out.

She went to Ruth's house next. The woman had no idea what her daughter-in-law was going to ask. "Mitchell is coming home tomorrow," she said.

"Could you stay with him during the day? It would really help."

Ruth stared at her, dumbfounded. "Have you talked to Mitchell about this?"

"He knows. He doesn't like the idea, but I didn't give him much say in the matter," she replied.

"He could stay here," Ruth said, groping for another solution.

"Ruth, think about what you're saying. You can't handle him alone," Megan told her mother-in-law gently, not wanting to hurt her feelings.

Ruth nodded. Without further debate, they made plans for the next day.

As soon as Megan got home, she called the children downstairs and blurted out the news.

"All right!" Zack shouted joyfully.

"You're not really letting him come here, are you?" Jess protested.

Megan addressed Jess. "What would you like me to do with him?"

"Let him go somewhere else," she snapped impatiently.

"Where? A nursing home or the street?" Megan asked calmly.

"I don't know. Let his family take care of him," she grumbled, not realizing what she was saying.

"Jess, we *are* his family. He's my husband and your father," she said gently. She let her words penetrate for a few minutes before she spoke again. "Will I be able to count on you for help?" She looked from one child to the other.

She got an instant response from Zack. "Anything, Mom."

Jess was trying to ignore her. "Can I count on you to help, Jess?" Megan asked.

"I guess," she sighed glumly.

Megan smiled at her compassionately, understanding how she felt. "Thanks, I knew I could count on you guys," she said.

Late that night in bed, Megan's wedding vows kept nagging at her. She got up and went to the family room. She opened the bottom of the bookcase and took out her wedding album. She sat down and slowly flipped through the pages. Why had their marriage gone sour? Had it been her fault?

The next morning everything seemed to go wrong. Jess was in a contrary mood. Megan dropped everything she touched. The phone at the shop wouldn't stop ringing.

By the time Ted arrived, she was rushing around like a wild woman. "What's going on?" he asked.

Megan stopped short and looked at him. "I'm bringing Mitchell home from the hospital this morning." She sighed.

"That's great! He couldn't have a better place to recover than with his family. How's he doing?" Ted asked, making it sound as if it were an expected turn of events.

Megan was so glad he hadn't asked if she had lost her mind. She relaxed a little. "Not so great. I think he's kind of depressed. He's not too happy with this move, either."

"I can understand that."

"You can? Then explain it to me. It may help!"

"From what you've told me, he came back hoping for a reconciliation. This isn't exactly what he had in mind.'' He looked at her thoughtfully. ''Are you happy with this?''

''This isn't exactly what I had in mind, either,'' she admitted. ''But it will all work out in the end, if we trust in God.'' Not wanting to talk about it anymore, she collected the flower arrangements she needed to deliver at the hospital, and hurried out.

Mitchell had already been discharged when she arrived. They politely said ''hello'' to one another, then a nurse wheeled him to the exit. It took both of them to help him into the van.

Mitchell slumped against the door and hardly said a word on the trip to the farm. Megan noticed that he tensed up every time she hit a bump or went around a curve. She slowed down. Poor guy! He was really hurting.

Ted was watching for them. When he saw the van drive up, he dashed out to help. ''Mitchell, good to see you,'' Ted said, opening the van door. ''Let me give you a hand,'' he said, taking him by the arm as Mitchell's legs buckled.

It took all their strength to get him to the top step. Mitchell was exhausted when they finally sat him on the bed.

''I better get back to work before the boss notices I'm gone,'' Ted kidded, hoping to lighten things up. Neither Mitchell nor Megan said a thing. ''Hope you're feeling better soon, Mitchell,'' Ted said, making his exit.

''Thanks,'' Mitchell mumbled.

Megan fussed about for a few minutes. Then she went to her room and snatched her portable TV off its shelf and hauled it to the guest room. After that she dashed downstairs and returned a few minutes later with some fruit juice. She held the straw to Mitch's mouth. "Here, try this. You look a little withered!"

He took a sip, not wanting to seem ungrateful by refusing. At the moment he didn't want anything, except to be left alone. Every inch of him seem to be screaming in pain. "Why did you bring me here?" he whispered.

Megan felt for him, he looked so defeated. She smiled at him wickedly, knowing things needed to lighten up a bit. "To torture you, of course."

He almost smiled. "I should have known."

She pulled the wooden rocker over to the bed and sat down. Rubbing her hands together with a sly gleam in her eyes, she said, "You see the way I have it figured, I'm a lousy nurse. So what better way to get back at you than to bring you here."

"You mean, I'm at your mercy?" he said, trying to go along with her plan to get his mind off the current circumstances.

"You got it." She smiled smugly, determined to keep things upbeat.

They heard the kitchen door open. Megan gave his covers a final straightening and gave him another sip of juice. He looked at her, troubled.

She knew what was on his mind. "Look, we're going to have plenty of time to talk. Right now the most important thing is for you to get well and for me to get back to work. I'll see you tonight. Rest, Mitchell!" she ordered as she hurried out.

Megan met Ruth on the landing and gave her an update and Doc's instructions. She thanked her and promised to get home as early as possible.

Then Megan dashed down the rest of the steps and out the door—running from her confused emotions.

Chapter Seven

Megan threw herself into work to keep her mind off her problems. By the end of the day she had potted and replanted everything, whether it needed it or not.

After locking the shop, Ted stood by his car watching Megan walk home. She stopped at the door, squared her shoulders, lifted her chin, then went inside. He knew she would make it.

Ruth was putting dinner on the table as she came in. She glanced around: the house was straight, too. "All I wanted you to do was take care of Mitch," Megan sighed, but it lifted her spirits knowing she had help.

"It was no trouble. I had to do something. Mitchell spent most of the day sleeping. Besides, since when is it a crime to give your family a little help?" Ruth asked.

"Believe me, I won't complain as long as you don't wear yourself out," Megan said.

"I fixed a tray for Mitchell," Ruth said, picking it up.

"Here, I'll take it up. You sit down and eat," Megan ordered.

Ruth smiled to herself and handed the tray to her daughter-in-law.

Upstairs Megan found Zack propped up on the bed beside his father. Jess was at the door watching them. "Dinner's ready," she said, standing aside as the children raced down the stairs.

"How was your day?" Megan asked Mitchell as she sat the tray on the nightstand. He managed a weak smile but didn't say anything.

Megan saw that he would need help eating. She gave him a hand sitting up, propping the pillows behind him. Nervously, she began spooning food into his mouth, wanting to get it over with. Mitchell slowed her down when she went too fast.

"I'm so sorry," she apologized.

"No, *I'm* sorry," he said in a hoarse voice. He knew she was tired and on edge.

"Shall we try again?" she said gently. Mitchell nodded.

When Ruth poked her head in the bedroom, everything seemed to be under control. "If you don't need me, I'm going home," she said, glad all was going well.

"Thanks for your help," Megan said, a little sorry to see her leave.

Ruth kissed Mitchell's forehead. "I left a plate in the oven for you, Megan. See you both in the morning."

"I'll get it later. Thanks," Megan replied, not really hungry.

Shortly, Zack came bounding up the stairs. "Mom, go eat. I'll stay with Dad."

Megan escaped to the kitchen, only to find Jess waiting for her. She had questions about her father. Someone had been telling her stories and she wanted her mother to confirm them.

"I'm going to my room," she said, leaving her mother in the wake of her unexpected inquisition.

Alone, Megan called her sister, suspecting she was the busybody. Cass answered the phone. "Have you been talking about Mitch to Jess?"

Her sister immediately went on the attack. "I heard you took him in. I can't believe you would do something so stupid," she raved. "Have you lost your mind? That man has never been anything but trash. Throw him out. How can you allow him to be around Jessica? And he's a bad influence on Zack," she screeched.

"Would you like me to throw him in the street or would you prefer I take him to the dump?" Megan asked sarcastically.

"Either one of those is fine with me. It's where he deserves to be. He has your sympathy because he's hurt. You were always dragging some injured animal home, trying to fix it up! Or helping someone out of a mess they made for themselves. How long will it be before he wants more than a faithful nurse, and makes a pass at you?"

"He's a human being and he needs help," Megan said staunchly.

"I know that. But you're still married to him. He'll try to take advantage of that, mark my word. I told you to divorce him. Wake up or he'll break your heart again. When he does, remember, I told you so," she lashed out.

"Do what you want with your life, Cass, but don't

tell my daughter any more gossip about her father. I'll tell her what she needs to know in my own time. Would you like someone telling your son every mistake you ever made?" Megan waited. Cass didn't answer. "I don't want you telling her any more. Do you understand?" Megan said and slammed the phone down.

Peeking in Jess's room, Megan found her almost asleep. "I love you," she said, hugging her girl.

Jess rolled over, yawning. "I love you, too."

She went to say goodnight to her son.

"Today worked out okay," Zack said positively.

"It's over," Megan answered wearily.

Then, reluctantly, she checked Mitchell. He was asleep. She tiptoed quietly in, turned off the lamp and plugged in a night-light.

At last Megan got in bed. She picked up her Bible. Faith in God had gotten her this far. He would see her through this too. She read until she got sleepy. Then she turned out the light.

The bout with Cass began to rerun in her mind. Cass had no right to turn Jess against her father. The child had enough to deal with, without knowing all Mitchell's mistakes and flaws.

During the night Megan woke to a strange noise. She got up to investigate and followed the sounds straight to the guest room. Mitchell was moaning in pain. Megan shook him gently. "Are you all right?"

His eyes opened sluggishly, then closed.

"What's wrong?" Megan whispered.

"Head hurts," he mumbled.

Megan went in the bathroom and found the prescription Doc had given her. "Here, take this," she said, popping a pill into his mouth and giving him a sip of water.

He moved again and cringed. "Anything else wrong?" she asked. He shook his head, but she wasn't convinced. "I can't help if I don't know what's wrong."

"You've done enough already," he murmured.

"Look, I didn't bring you here to make you suffer," she said crisply. "I really want to help."

His eyes opened slowly. "You're tired."

She smiled slightly. "True, and I'm not in the mood for guessing games. So do you want to tell me what's wrong, so we can both get some rest?"

He frowned. "My back really hurts. I guess lying around all day tensed it up."

It was no wonder. A nurse would give him a back rub. She'd accepted this job, she would see it through. Efficiently she rolled him on his side. Then she smoothed lotion on his back and gently began to massage his shoulders and back. She could feel him relaxing.

After she was sure he was asleep, she propped some extra pillows behind him and went back to bed.

The next day things went a little more smoothly. But late that night Mitchell was once again plagued with the same symptoms. Megan repeated the treatment of the night before, this time a little more comfortable with the job.

The next night Megan decided to try the preventive approach. After she tucked Jess in bed, she went to the guest room. Zack was keeping his father company. Megan stood at the door, looking in. "I just came by to see if you need anything," she said.

"I'm fine," Mitchell said, trying to smile convincingly.

Zack hopped up and offered her the rocking chair. "I'm on the way to my room. Why don't you sit down for a minute? You look tired."

Megan accepted the offer. She glanced around to see if anything needed straightening. Eventually, her eyes came to rest on Mitchell. "How are you?"

"So-so," he admitted.

"I thought I'd give you a back rub now, if you don't mind," she said shyly.

"I don't mind," he said, giving her a crooked little smile.

After she finished her duties, she fluffed the pillows and tucked him in. For the past three days they had said very little to one another.

"Stay for a minute," Mitchell said, knowing she was about to bolt. "I didn't want to come here. I know this isn't fair to you."

"It was the only choice," Megan answered, hoping he wouldn't question her.

"How do you figure that?" he asked, a bit stunned. She didn't answer. "Why, Megan?"

"We're your family," she said quietly.

"And you don't turn your back on your family. Not like I did," he said.

"I didn't mean for it to sound like that. It's just... how could I..."

"You don't owe me anything. I don't want anything from you," he said softly.

She glanced at her tensely clasped hands. "I know."

"But you still feel responsible?" he asked, confused.

This conversation was coming too close to things that hurt deeply. She nodded once. "Meg, you don't have to do this. I can go to a nursing home or hire someone to stay with me. I'm not your problem.''

"No matter what's wrong between us, this is your family. It's not right to turn our backs on one another. I did what I believe is right," she said assuredly.

"Doc told me this was your decision. Is that true?"

"Yes," she said, her tone stubborn.

"Did you ask the kids or Mom first?" he asked.

"No." The pain medication was taking effect; she wished it would hurry.

"Why didn't you divorce me while I was gone?" he asked. His speech was getting slow as he fought to keep his eyes open.

"You want a divorce—you get it!" she whispered bitterly.

He couldn't seem to hold his eyes open. They batted several times before sliding closed. "I don't want one either," he sighed.

Megan was glad he was asleep. "Sleep well," she murmured.

Friday night Zack had a date and Jess was going roller skating with a friend. After the children left, Megan went to check on the patient. The TV was playing as he dozed. She turned to leave.

"Meg," he called.

"I thought you were sleeping."

"Just a nap. What are you doing?"

"Well, there are tons of things that need doing, but I thought I'd see if you wanted some company," she said hesitantly.

He smiled slightly. "Anytime. Is Zack still here?"

"No. He left a while ago."

"Could you help me get up?" he asked, looking a

little embarrassed. Usually Zack was there to help him to the bathroom, which left him with a little dignity.

"Sure," Megan said easily and helped him to the bathroom door.

She straightened up the room a bit while she waited for him. When he came hobbling out, she went to his aid. He draped his arm around her shoulder for support. "You know we're alone tonight," he said, trying to keep his balance.

"I was warned you'd make a pass," she shot back at him.

"Your sister?"

"Yep."

"I imagine she said 'Throw the bum out,'" he said candidly.

"That's pretty accurate," Megan admitted, steadying him. "So, is this it?" she teased.

"Best I can do." He grinned, as she helped him back into bed. She took a seat in the rocker. "Why don't you sit over here?" He nodded toward the empty side of the bed.

"I don't think so." She laughed.

"I just thought maybe you'd watch an old movie with me. That chair must be kind of hard on your back. Look, we'd have a broken arm between us." He held up the proof.

Megan was tired and the thought of sitting in the rocker through a movie was not comforting. Against her better judgment, she accepted his offer and sat on the bed.

During the commercials they talked. "Ever taken your rings off?" he asked casually.

Megan lifted her hand, admiring the rings. "The diamond, when I make meat loaf. It gets stuck underneath. You?'' she asked, glancing at Mitchell's wedding ring.

''Nope, never,'' he said. He watched her expression.

''Let's see if you have the groove!'' Megan reached over and gently felt his finger. She could feel the impression left from constantly wearing the ring.

''The groove?'' He frowned, feeling under his ring. He'd never noticed it before. ''Have you got the groove?'' he asked, reaching for her hand.

She hesitated at first, then held out her left hand. As he felt the indentation, he watched her intently. ''Why did you bother to wait?''

She flashed him a surprised look. ''It wasn't a question of waiting. It had to do with the vows. The promises to God and…'' She couldn't finish.

''Wish I hadn't come back?'' Mitchell asked, releasing her hand.

She refused to answer, looking for a way to change the subject. ''What happened the night you got beat up? I heard kids and drugs were involved. Would you care to explain?'' she asked, suddenly sounding as if this were a cross-examination.

''Not really. I didn't do anything wrong. I was trying to help someone in trouble,'' he said defensively.

''I heard the police questioned you!''

''They did,'' he said calmly.

Fear suddenly engulfed Megan. ''If you're involved in anything that will hurt my children, I'll throw you out so fast—''

He cut her off. ''I'm not,'' he said, irritated. ''Just take my word for it.''

Staring angrily at one another like two cats with their backs bristled, each waited for the other to make the next move. Mitchell made another blunder by trying to change the subject. "How's your business doing?"

Cass's warning echoed in Megan's head.

As she glared at him warily, it dawned on Mitchell what she was thinking. "I can't believe you think I came back to steal your business and ruin our kids!" he said incredulously. "I have news for you. I came back because I love those kids, regardless of what you or anyone else thinks. As far as your business goes, I want no part of it. I was simply asking a question." He scrambled and wiggled until he was on his feet. Then he started wobbling toward the door. His face was filled with fury and disappointment.

His head began to spin, and Megan caught him just before his legs gave out. "Leave me alone! I want to get out of here. I don't need you or your charity. I don't need—" He choked on his words as his strength failed him. Feeling beaten, he quit fighting.

Megan steadied him with her arms. He didn't need this kind of turmoil any more than she did. "Right, as if you could get downstairs by yourself," she said, trying to kid him past this discord. "I'd have to roll you back up here step by step. Now you don't want to do that, do you?" She looked up at him.

"I'll call someone to come get me. I don't want to stay here if that's how you feel," he said. His eyes were watery.

"Mitchell," she said patiently. "You're not going anywhere but back to bed."

"You don't want me here!"

She nudged him a little and started leading him back to bed. When he was settled, she stood over him with her hands on her hips. "Why don't you let me make up my own mind?" Having said that, she left the room.

A while later she returned with two cups of tea. She

knew he hated the stuff, but it soothed *her*. She sat on
the vacant side of the bed and offered him a mug.

"Sure," he replied. "I forgot you promised to abuse
me."

"Torture, not abuse," she corrected with a gleam in
her eyes. They sat back and pretended to concentrate
on the movie.

When Mitchell finished the tea, he felt better. He
chanced looking at Megan. "I've never felt so humil-
iated in my whole life. To come back, after all this
time, and wind up under your roof this way is a real
blow to my fragile ego," he admitted.

"I know," Megan said softly, gently brushing her
knuckles over his cheek, which hadn't been shaved
since he'd been hurt. "You could use a shave."

His eyes lit up at her touch. "I'm sorry," he apologized.

"Me, too," she said, withdrawing her hand.

Mitchell settled back. He couldn't stand another confrontation. He dozed off, while Megan watched the
movie.

Jess came running up the stairs and stopped short at
the guest room. "Mom!" she wailed and fled to her
room. Megan jumped up, following her. The child
flung herself across her bed facedown.

"Jess, what's wrong?" Megan asked concerned.

"You were in bed with him!"

Megan was flabbergasted. "Jess, I was watching a
movie. I was on the bed, and he was asleep!"

"I don't want him here," she moaned.

Megan took her daughter in her arms. "I know this
is hard on you, but sometimes we have to do things
we'd rather not. Sometimes God tells us what He wants
us to do. We have to be faithful. I would never do

anything purposely to hurt you, you're just going to have to trust me on this. Okay?"

Jess wiped her eyes and nodded. "Can I watch TV with you for a little while?" Then she remembered that Mitch had possession of her mother's TV. "Never mind. I think I'll just go to bed," she said pitifully.

Megan gave her a kiss. "Sleep well, my baby girl." In the hallway she leaned against the wall, feeling torn. When she peeked in the guest room, she found Mitchell wide-awake.

"Problems?" he inquired.

Megan came in and sat down in the rocker. She needed to talk. "Jess thinks she caught me in bed with you."

Mitchell laughed at the absurdity of it.

"You know this is serious to her. And I feel like I got caught doing something wrong," she sputtered.

"I'm sorry she's upset, Meg, but do you think it would be better for her to believe we love each other, or the opposite?" he asked seriously.

"Depends on which is true," she said solemnly. Then she tucked him in for the night.

The next morning Megan woke Zack before she left for work. "Would you do me a favor before you come to work, and help your father with a bath and a shave?"

"Sure, sure," Zack murmured, covering his head with the sheet.

When Megan got home from work, Jess was still sour-faced. While they were eating lunch Cass called, inviting Jess to go shopping.

Jess had spent the morning with her father and was in a fractious mood. Megan figured Cass was in for a good dose of the "little angel," as she called her.

It was after two before Megan went to check on the patient. "You look much better," she said, trying to put the cross words from the night before behind them. "So, what would you like to do today?"

"Get out of this room," he blurted out.

"Cabin fever?" He nodded. "I'll see what I can do." She came back a few minutes later with Zack. The two of them helped him down the stairs.

He glanced around. "This is great."

Just before Zack went out, he asked his mother, "Do you want me to help you get Dad back upstairs?"

"He'll be okay. Don't be too late," she replied.

Megan fixed soup and sandwiches for dinner and they watched the news as they ate in silence. The wall was building between them.

When Mitchell finally looked over at Megan, she was asleep. Her hand was stretched across the sofa. It looked almost as though she was reaching for him. He put his hand over hers and gently wove their fingers together. A tear trickled down her cheek as she lightly squeezed his hand.

At length she looked at him, searching for answers to unasked questions. Mitchell slowly pulled their intertwined hands to him, drawing her closer. She tried to keep from trembling, but failed. Mitchell slipped his arm around her.

Against her better judgment, Megan let ten years of held-back tears erupt. She had been brave and lonely for such a long time. When Mitchell had taken off, she had lost not only her husband, but her best friend as well.

Mitchell held her and let her cry it out. He knew the depth of her pain; he himself had felt it often. There were no words, yet both understood.

Chapter Eight

Megan remained in Mitchell's arms until she heard the kitchen door open. Then she quickly moved away, wiping her eyes.

Jess came in the family room looking for her mother. She stopped when she saw Mitchell. "You brought him downstairs!" she exclaimed.

"What did you think? That he would be confined to quarters for the duration?" Megan laughed, then looked from Jess to Mitchell.

Mitchell could tell his daughter wasn't overjoyed that he had invaded the rest of the house. He supposed that if he were in her place, he'd feel the same way.

Megan jumped up and went to the bookshelf. She got down the Chinese checkers board, placed it in the middle of the sofa, and set it up. Jess loved to play and she was good at it. "Let's play a game," Megan suggested.

Her daughter and Mitch looked at the board and shrugged in agreement. Jess took a seat at the end of the sofa, glaring at her father. Megan sat on the coffee table, giving her a bird's-eye view of the action on and off the board.

Each turn, Jess and Mitchell eyed one another before they made a move. It came down to a close game: Jess won by one move. They played another game. This time Mitchell won by a narrow margin.

When they decided to play again, Megan bowed out. Game after game it went back and forth. Jess won the last game, and Mitchell proclaimed her the official champion. She grinned broadly, accepting the honor bestowed upon her.

Megan noticed Mitchell was looking whipped in more ways than one. "Think you could help me get your dad upstairs?" Megan asked Jess.

"Sure. He needs rest after the whippin' he took," she said pompously.

Mitchell laughed at the arrogance of his daughter. "Of course I expect a rematch," he challenged her.

"Any time. Any place," she said, her conceit remaining in place.

They started for the stairs. It wasn't quite as easy as Megan had expected. Mitchell was tired and his strength was zapped.

Halfway up, Mitchell felt like lying down on the steps. If they ever got him to the top, he was never coming down again. At last they reached the last step. Once he was steady, Jess started to retreat. "How about a rematch tomorrow?" he called after her.

"You bombed out, but if you want to play again, I'm game," Jess said, watching him hobble to the bathroom.

Megan followed Jess to her room. "What did Cass have to say?" Megan probed.

Jess frowned. "Nothing much."

Megan knew Cass talked nonstop. Jess just didn't want to talk about it.

"I'm going to bed," Jess said, dutifully kissing her mother. She watched her leave, knowing she would go to Mitch. She quietly eased herself into the hall and over next to the guest room door. She peeked around the corner.

Her mother touched Mitch's forehead with the back of her hand, the same way she did when she wasn't feeling well. Then she covered him and asked if he needed anything—the same way she did for her. It was disgusting. Jess tiptoed back to her room.

Megan was about to exit the room, when Mitchell asked if they could talk. "Can it wait until tomorrow?" she asked.

"No," he said firmly. Megan dropped into the chair beside the bed, looking guilty.

"We weren't doing anything wrong when Jess came in," he reminded her.

"I know it upsets her," she replied.

He held out his hand to her. Feeling challenged, she took it. "This?" he asked.

She closed her eyes wearily. "You just don't understand."

"Then explain it to me."

"It's not just upsetting Jess. *I'm* upset. All of a sudden, you're here. I've been alone for ten years. I've learned to trust God and myself."

He knew she was telling him that she didn't trust him anymore. He brushed his thumb across her hand as they studied one another.

Megan was lost in thought when she heard Zack's voice behind her. She jumped and tried to retrieve her hand.

Zack started chuckling. "Mom, it's okay with me if you hold Dad's hand, but I wouldn't let Jess catch you." Mitchell laughed, too.

"Very funny!" Megan said, turning crimson and pulling her hand free. "I don't need to be ganged up on," she said sharply, escaping to her room.

Trying to get to sleep, she heard occasional laughter coming from the guest room. Zack was so happy with this arrangement. But her own feelings were going up and down like a freight elevator. There were things she wanted to know…needed to know. Things she was afraid to ask.

She looked at the empty place beside her—the place where Mitchell used to belong. She felt anger rising in her. She reached over and smacked the pillow next to her. Then she turned away and went to sleep.

In the morning, Megan was still feeling the residue of her anger. She decided to leave Zack with his father while she and Jess went to church.

As soon as Megan arrived, Cass came charging at her. She gave Cass a quick hug and waved at her nephew, Brian, who was standing at a distance from his mother. He gave her a thin smile and waved back. "How's the family, Cassie?" she asked quickly, thinking that if she could get her sister talking about herself, she would forget everything else.

"Fine. My family is just fine," she snapped. "How long do you intend to keep this up? Jess is miserable. She told me how awful things are at home. Poor child! How could you do this to her? It's not fair! I can't believe you would put his welfare ahead of your own daughter's," she fumed.

"Life isn't always fair. Jess might as well find out

now," Megan answered evenly. "The service is about to start, we'd better find a seat," Megan said, catching Jess by the hand and dragging her along. Jess followed sheepishly, knowing she was in trouble.

Cass had stepped over the line. Now she was undermining Megan in front of Jess. Megan tried to concentrate on the service, but her thoughts kept drifting as she reviewed her problems over and over again.

Megan and Jess rode home in mutual silence, each upset with the other. As they pulled in the driveway, a large, black man was coming out of the house. He said "hello" and continued to his car and drove away.

Megan hurried inside. The guest room floor was cluttered with boxes and across them was a pile of clothes on hangers. "What's all this?" she asked abruptly.

"The place I've been living needed my room for someone else," he told her.

"You've been evicted!" Her voice rang out in the room.

"Not exactly. They needed the space," he explained feebly.

"So they bring your stuff and dump it here! Didn't you tell them you were coming back?" she cried.

"Mom, what are you getting so upset about? It's just a couple of boxes and a few clothes," Zack pointed out.

She knew she wasn't handling this very well. "I don't know. I'm sorry. Let me get this stuff off the floor." She hung the clothes in the closet. Then she opened the first box and started putting things in the dresser.

In the last box, she found an old worn Bible. She turned to Mitchell. "Is this the one your mother gave you for graduation?" He nodded. She opened it. The

Bible was all marked and written in; it looked much like her own. She handed it to Zack. "Put it by the bed."

She continued to unpack the box until she came to an old sweatshirt with something wrapped inside. She carefully unfolded it and found a framed picture of herself, very pregnant, holding Zack on her lap.

She stared at the old photograph in shock. It had been protected like a treasure. She quickly wrapped it again and placed it back in the box. "Maybe you should go through this yourself," she said, slid it into the closet, and rushed out.

Zack hadn't seen what his mother had uncovered. He looked at his father, puzzled. "What's wrong with her?"

"Take a look," Mitchell told him.

Zack went to the closet and looked in the box. He was almost as stunned as his mother had been. "You kept it all this time?"

"It was all I had," Mitchell said with a faraway look.

Zack carried the picture with him and sat on the bed near his father. "You know, I remember the day you took this picture. We were at the park and it started raining. You put your jacket around Mom and you picked me up and we all ran to the car, laughing." They stared at one another, realizing Megan must have remembered too.

"Do you think you could help me get downstairs?" Mitch asked.

"Sure," Zack said.

Megan was setting the table for lunch when they came into the kitchen.

"I thought I'd come down and save some of the

running," Mitchell said, trying to sound casual, instead of out of breath. He tried not to grimace as he sat in the straight-back chair.

Jess came hurrying in when her mother called. She skidded to a halt when she found Mitch already at the table.

Mitchell said the blessing. Then the meal proceeded in troubled silence. After a decent amount of time passed, Megan began clearing the table. "Zack, don't you think your dad would be more comfortable in the family room?" she suggested gently, noticing Mitch was looking stiff.

Jess helped her mother clean up. Then curiosity led her to see what Zack and her father were doing. Zack had a photo album on his lap, and was showing Mitch the pictures.

Jess went to the arm of the sofa and stood watching them. Before long she moved a little closer, helping Zack with the picture details.

Megan noticed the album and just wasn't up to a trip down memory lane. "I need to go out and get something," she said, addressing no one in particular. Without looking up, they all gave some sort of agreeable answer.

Megan rode toward town. She stopped at the park, where the picture she'd uncovered earlier had been taken, and got out.

Young couples were walking hand in hand. Children were feeding the greedy ducks. Babies were being pushed in strollers. Groups of children were playing tag and baseball. Megan walked to the picnic table under a large tree, and sat down.

An empty place in her chest seemed to be growing,

plunging into the depths of her soul. This was the spot where Mitch had asked her to marry him.

Marry me, Meg, be my wife, he had said. Where had it all gone wrong? She had loved him so much. She'd never loved another man—only him.

Sitting in that spot, she remembered the joy she had felt that night. She was so happy. She believed she could make him happy forever. But she'd failed. As she looked up, a young couple with a little boy was coming her way.

Megan jumped up and ran to the van. She drove aimlessly, trying to stop crying, but the tears continued to roll. She didn't want to go home like this.

After stopping in the church parking lot, she tried the front door, and found it unlocked. She slipped into a pew in the back of the church. Within minutes she was engulfed in memories of them standing at the altar, making their vows. She was staring into Mitch's eyes, unashamed, promising. She heard the words, *I Megan, take thee Mitchell…until death do us part.*

"End my misery. Please God, help me," she begged, crying harder than before.

The front door opening startled her. She quickly wiped her eyes, then looked around. It was the minister, John Goodwin.

"Megan, I saw your van out front. Is everything all right?" Reverend Goodwin asked, sliding into the pew in front of her.

"I don't know. It's a lot of things," she said, fighting to keep her raw emotions in check. She knew he noticed her tear-stained face; there was no way to hide it.

"I heard you took your husband in after his accident.

That was a very kind thing to do. How is he?'' he asked sincerely.

"Improving. He's on his feet a little. Actually, he's made a lot of progress,'' she said, glad to have someone to talk to who wasn't condemning her.

"I imagine this is very difficult for all of you,'' Reverend Goodwin empathized.

Megan nodded, not trusting her voice.

"You know, sometimes we're tested. We say a lot of things that sound good, but when the test comes, we find whether we really can stand by our word, or if we fall away. What's right is not always the easy thing to do. Sometimes it's the hardest. God will guide you— if you let Him.''

"How do I do that? I'm so confused. Everyone wants me to do things their way. I feel pulled in a lot of different directions at once,'' she admitted.

"Who is it most important to please?'' Reverend Goodwin asked.

Megan looked at him, not understanding what he meant.

"You can't please everyone. You must decide who comes first,'' he said lightly, as though it wasn't a hard decision at all. "Think about it. The answer will come to you,'' he said confidently.

They talked for a few more minutes. Then they rose and walked out of the church together. Reverend Goodwin patted her shoulder. "Trust in God. He has the answers,'' he said, and walked away.

Megan sat in the van for a few more minutes, thinking about what the minister had said. She was trying to listen to God, but everyone else seemed to be drowning out His voice.

At home, she found Jess and Mitchell having a Chinese checkers rematch. Megan's eyes met Mitchell's for a split second. He looked worn-out.

Mitch could tell that she had been crying. He wanted to reach out to her, but it wasn't the right time.

Suddenly, Jess remembered that she had a bug collection due the next day. In near hysteria, she begged Zack to help her find the needed insects. The two hurried out the door in a mad rush.

Megan dropped on the opposite end of the sofa. She leaned back and closed her eyes. She'd always been a fighter, not inclined to giving up. Everything would work out.

The kids came hurrying back into the house, and the door slammed behind them. Megan's eyes flew open; she realized she had fallen asleep.

"Can we go get pizza?" Zack whispered when he saw his father asleep.

Megan nodded sleepily and pointed to her pocketbook. Zack got money for the food, and they tiptoed out.

As the truck pulled away, Mitchell whispered, "You awake?"

"Um-hum," Megan mumbled with her eyes closed.

"I'm sorry I upset you today," he said quietly.

"I'll survive."

"Why are you avoiding me?" he asked.

Megan's heart beat rapidly. She felt as though she'd been caught doing something wrong again. "I needed some time alone, to think," she replied.

"The picture upset you," he pried.

"I just wasn't expecting it."

"Sometimes we get what we don't expect. Right, Meg?"

She opened her eyes and looked over at him. "What

have you gotten that you didn't expect?'' she asked curiously.

''My family, giving me the best of care,'' he said tenderly.

His comment almost broke her heart. Raw emotions surfaced once more and tears rose quickly in her throat. She bowed her head, ashamed of herself.

''Meg, we were looking for a second chance before all this happened. Can't we start there again?'' Mitch asked.

She began trembling. Mitchell put his feet down, scooted closer to her, and slipped his arm around her.

''I'm sorry. I don't know what's wrong with me today,'' she said, dabbing at her eyes.

''I'm here if you need me.''

''You weren't before.'' She continued to sniff.

''People change.''

''Do they?'' She looked at him.

''Haven't you—over the years?''

She wanted to escape, but something in his eyes held her captive. ''Have I?''

''Definitely. You have it all together. You're a great mother. You run a thriving business. You haven't compromised yourself or your beliefs to get there. You've proved you can make it against the odds,'' Mitchell said proudly.

Megan felt like a fool sitting there listening to him. Her face was covered with drying tears, she had experienced an afternoon of insanity, and she couldn't seem to make up her mind about anything. She felt totally inept with the man beside her. ''I failed horribly as a wife,'' she said, and her head sagged forward.

''Never,'' he said confidently. ''If it hadn't been for you, I'd be dead. I would have given up long ago.''

"Don't say that!"

"It's true. I got to a place where I just wanted to die," he said solemnly.

She looked at him, shocked. "Is that true? Why?"

"Because I couldn't stand myself anymore. I'd become a person I hated. I hated the way I was living and the things I was doing. I hated it all, but I was too weak and powerless to change my ways. So I wanted to die. I thought it would be the easy way out. But I kept thinking about you. And I couldn't let go."

Before he could say any more, the truck pulled up. Megan wiped her eyes again. She glanced at Mitch, not sure what she was feeling. She hated the way the world was tearing at her. She understood some of how he felt.

"I need you," he pleaded, and held her to him for a moment. Then, not wanting to embarrass her again, he moved away before the children came in.

That night when the house was quiet, Megan crept upstairs, assuming everyone was asleep. The lamp was still on in the guest room. She tiptoed in to turn it off.

"Aren't you going to say anything?" Mitch asked, startling her.

She knew he was referring to his earlier disclosure. "I don't know what to say. What do you expect me to say? I thought we would have time to get to know one another again. I didn't expect…this," she answered honestly.

"Having second thoughts about taking in the prodigal husband?"

"No! Only about keeping him," she returned.

"Why?" he asked, shocked that keeping him had even crossed her mind.

"I trusted you before."

"And I broke that trust. So you'll never trust me again. Is that what you're saying?" he asked.

"I don't know if I can," she admitted.

"When do you think you'll be able to make that decision?"

"I don't know. Why are you pushing me?" They stared at one another for a moment.

"I love you. What am I supposed to do?" he finally asked, venting his frustration.

Briskly, Megan turned the light out, angry that he thought he was being inconvenienced by waiting for her. She had waited years for him. She marched to the door, steaming mad, then stopped and looked back at him. "Prove it!" she said, dead serious, and walked out.

Chapter Nine

Prove it! Mitchell dwelt on Megan's demand. How was he supposed to prove he loved her? He'd stopped drinking. He'd literally pulled himself out of the gutter for her. Couldn't she see that?

Megan's words, *It will all work out, if we just hold on and trust God to help us,* had carried him through unbearable times. Now she questioned everything. His honesty, his integrity…his love. On top of all that, she wanted proof that he loved her. Love was intangible. How was he supposed to prove it?

Mitchell lay in bed wondering how she had come to the conclusion he no longer loved her. Once he thought about it, the answer was pretty obvious. He hadn't had the courage to talk to her the whole time he was gone.

He did call occasionally. He would wait for her to answer and repeatedly say "hello," then he would hang up. He told himself he left because he loved her and didn't want to ruin her life. In looking back, he knew he had taken the coward's way out.

She had no idea how hard it had been for him to

come and face her. He remembered how she'd reacted. She hadn't been expecting him to come back. Had she given up?

He tried to put himself in her place. Waiting, expecting—something, anything. Then day after day, year after year, not a word. It looked pretty bleak, even to him.

The kicker was that now she was taking care of him. That was the unexpected little twist Mitchell hadn't counted on.

No longer trusting her feelings, Megan was waiting for something to show her what was right. Mitch wanted it all to be so easy. But it wasn't easy. It had been ten long, hard and lonely years. For him to come back and say he'd changed didn't prove a thing. Neither did his denial of any wrongdoing the night he was beaten. She needed him to show her something solid to hold on to and believe.

Trouble was brewing. Megan could feel its approach, like the still before a storm. Then one afternoon she came home to find a police car parked by the house. She expected at any second to see Mitchell being hauled out in handcuffs. She burst into the kitchen and found Mitchell serving coffee to two officers. She stopped in her tracks.

"They haven't come to take me away yet," Mitchell said, laughing a little too loudly. "This is my wife, Megan. This is Rich and Dan, a couple of friends."

Both men shook hands with Megan. She quickly apologized for the intrusion and escaped to her room, where she found Jess flopped across her bed.

"Have the cops taken him away yet?" she asked sarcastically.

"No, I don't think they're here to do anything like that."

"Rats! I thought maybe we were getting rid of him!"

"Jessica, this is your father you're talking about," Megan said, shocked.

"Oh, right. I forgot—since I grew up without him. He never wanted me. He left before I was even born. He never came to see me or even sent me a lousy card. So why should I care what happens to him?" she said, the years of hurt showing.

Megan sat on the bed. "Regardless of what you think, Jess, he does love you. He didn't leave because of you. He left because I told him to. If you need to blame someone, blame me. And he did send you money. He sent it to Gran, and I wouldn't accept it. Ask her. She has it all put away for you. He cares about you. I'm sure of it."

"Well, I don't need him and I never will. I'll be glad when he's gone," she said, looking at her mother for confirmation. Her mother didn't answer. "Don't tell me he's staying!"

"I didn't say that. Although he'll always be your father. You can't change that. He's trying. It wouldn't hurt for you to do the same. He made a mistake leaving before you were born. He's trying to make up for the past."

"Maybe the cops will decide to take him anyway," she said hopefully.

"Let's go see," Megan said, thinking maybe it would do her daughter good to see that the police officers were friends of her father.

The officers were about to leave as Jess peeked in the kitchen. "Who's this?" Dan asked.

"This is my daughter, Jess," Mitchell replied proudly.

"Nice to meet you," both officers said. "Guess you're glad to have your dad home," Rich said.

Jess just stared at him, wondering why she would be glad.

"Nice to meet both of you," he said.

"Take care of yourself, Mitchell. We appreciate your help," Rich added.

Mitchell opened the door for them. As soon as they were gone, he turned to Megan with a grim expression.

Zack pulled in the driveway as the police car was leaving. "What's up?" he asked as he came in the kitchen.

"The cops came for him!" Jess bellowed.

Zack laughed, thinking she was kidding. Then looked at his parents. Something was wrong. "Come on, you can tell me all about it," he said, leading her to his room.

Mitchell continued to glare at Megan. "You really thought they'd come to get me! You should have seen your face. You're just waiting for me to slip up, aren't you?

"You don't want to make a decision because you don't really believe I've changed. I guess you figure if you wait long enough, I'll screw up and the decision will be made for you. That's it, isn't it, Megan. Well, I'm human. I'm bound to make a few mistakes along the way. So if you're just waiting for me to mess up, I may as well leave now. Are you ever going to forgive me?" he asked, disheartened.

"I have forgiven you. I brought you here," she said, defending herself weakly.

"That was charity. You may think you've forgiven

me, but you haven't. You've said it, but in your heart I'm still guilty as charged," he said sternly.

He made his way past her and climbed the stairs slowly, closing the guest room door behind himself.

Megan slumped into a chair. She had been assaulted by his words because there was some truth to them. She hadn't expected him to see through her hesitation. She didn't want to make any more mistakes, she'd made enough already.

After fixing dinner for the children, she took a tray to the guest room and found the door closed. She knocked lightly, then opened the door when there was no reply. Mitchell was lying across the bed, facedown.

"I brought you some dinner," she said quietly, putting the tray on the nightstand. He didn't respond. She knew if she walked out, she would be responsible for the consequences.

Megan sat down heavily on the bed. "I'm sorry, Mitch. You're right, I don't trust you. You haven't given me any reason to. You just showed up and expected everything to fall into place. Do you have any idea how it feels to have someone you love walk out on you?" she asked.

Not talking things out had always been one of their problems. Megan knew it was time to change that. She propped herself on her elbow alongside him. "Talk to me, Mitch," she whispered, smoothing his hair while she waited. He rubbed his face on his sleeve and turned slowly to face her. "I'm trying," she apologized.

"Is it that hard?" he asked, searching her eyes.

"Yes. If you had just called once in a while, but there was nothing."

"I was trying to let you be free," he defended himself.

"Free? You think I was free? I was tormented. I drove you away."

"No! It wasn't your fault. So stop blaming yourself," he said sharply. He could see that she didn't understand. "You told me if I left, not to come back until I was straight—so I didn't."

"How do I know that's true?"

"You don't. You have to trust me," Mitchell said, raising his eyebrows.

"You don't make it easy. You don't tell me anything," she reprimanded him.

"No matter what I tell you, you still have to decide if you believe me."

"You could make it a little easier," Megan said.

Mitch knew this stalemate needed to end. "Tell me how, and I will."

"I get a call. You're in the hospital. I find out it has to do with you, kids and drugs. No one will tell me anything. You're half-dead. I bring you home, not knowing what to expect. Then I come home today and find a police car here. Now what would *you* think?" she said.

"I see your point. If I tell you the truth, will you believe me? No questions asked?"

"Just give me a chance," she begged.

"Okay. The night I got beaten up, I went to help a friend who was in trouble with his drug supplier. He'd been selling their stuff and spending their money. They were threatening him. He was scared and had every right to be. Drug suppliers are deadly serious about their money.

"I knew they might hurt him, so I went with him. They start with fear tactics, such as threats. If that doesn't get action, pain and suffering are next. If that doesn't work, they kill you. Since I came along, instead of hurting him, they decided to make an example out of me. Understand?''

Megan was stunned by his disclosure.

Jess happened by the door about that time. Her mother and Mitch were lying across the bed, staring at one another. She stepped to the side of the door, out of sight.

''So you're telling me you were on the side of the drug dealer—not the supplier,'' she said disappointedly.

''It's not that simple, Meg. I know the kid who was selling. He's about Zack's age. He's not a bad kid. He's just neglected. He got in over his head. He had no idea these guys would kill him for a few bucks without batting an eye. I was trying to save his neck.''

''That's all you're going to tell me?'' she asked.

''Yep. You either believe me or you don't. I'm not going to verify it for you.''

''But you could?''

''If I broke a confidence—yes. But I'm not going to do that.''

''I'm not sure why, but I believe you,'' she said thoughtfully.

Mitch smiled hesitantly.

''Is Jess upset? She hasn't had much to say to me lately. I guess she'd like me to go back where I came from,'' he admitted sadly. ''I love her so much. I wish I could make her understand.''

Jess had heard enough. She came to the door, pretending she had just gotten there. ''Mom, can I go to a school skate tomorrow night? One of my friends can take me.''

''When you get home from school, do your homework and chores and stay off the phone. I'll let you know when I get home," she answered. Recently Jess had been leaving her chores undone and spending the afternoons on the phone.

"Why can't you tell me now?" Jess demanded.

"Because I haven't made up my mind."

"Would it help if I stared at you?" Jess retorted, and stomped off.

Megan knew she'd been listening. It didn't matter at this point. Right now she and Mitchell needed to finish clearing the air. "You know we never talked things out before. You yelled, I yelled and neither one of us listened to the other. We both wanted to be right," she recollected.

"I didn't care if I was right. I just wanted my own way," he admitted.

"I wanted mine too. Everything wasn't your fault. I was a lot to blame. I expected you to make me happy," she confessed.

"I expected you to keep me from self-destruction!"

"I guess we failed one another," she said, feeling let down.

"I'm not so sure of that. I didn't self-destruct. You did your part." He waited to see what she would say.

Her eyes avoided his. "I've had a lot of happy times."

"Then we aren't complete failures," he said, wanting everything to be right between them, though they had more rough spots to face. "I knew I couldn't come back unless I had cleaned up my life. I want my family more than anything," he admitted, reaching out and gently touching her cheek, smiling hopefully.

Megan stared at him wide-eyed, afraid to admit that she might want the same thing.

* * *

The next evening Megan came in from work to find the house in complete silence. She wandered into the family room and found Mitchell sitting on the sofa, staring at his feet. She sat down on the coffee table, facing him. "Anything wrong?"

"You could say that. Jessica is up in her room crying," he said, sounding forlorn.

"Why?"

"She stayed on the phone all afternoon. She didn't do her homework or anything else. I guess I over-reacted," he admitted guiltily.

"And?" Megan pressed.

"I told her to get off the phone. She got mad and yelled at me. I told her she wasn't going out tonight and that she was grounded for a week. She's been in her room crying ever since." He looked unclear about his position.

"Welcome to parenthood," Megan said seriously.

"She hates me!"

Megan bit her lip. It was time he knew some of the things Jess had been thinking. "She believes she's the reason you left, that you never wanted her or cared about her. So she's determined to reject you equally."

"You don't believe that, do you?" he asked, aston-ished.

"No, but at one time or another all of us have felt responsible for your leaving."

"It was me. It had nothing to do with any of you," he said, troubled.

"To Jess, you left right before she was born. There-fore she feels you didn't want her. She needs to know you really love her, even when she's rotten," Megan pointed out.

"How do I do that?" he asked, looking discon-
certed.

"That's something you're going to have to figure out
for yourself. Right now, I'm going up to have a little
talk with her," she said. She was not looking forward
to the encounter. She was caught in the middle and
feeling squeezed.

Megan knocked lightly on Jess's closed door.

"Who is it?" she growled.

"Mom."

The door opened quickly and Jess flew into her
mother's arms. "Mom, he's so mean," she cried. "I
was getting off the phone. I told him he didn't have
any right telling me what to do. I'd be glad when he's
gone. I hate him." Then she went on describing her fit
of temper. To her, Mitchell was to blame, even though
she had completely ignored her mother's instructions.
She began to cry as though she was a helpless victim.

"Stop it, Jess," Megan ordered, leading her daughter
into her room.

"I'm sorry, Mom. I'm really sorry. I meant to do
my homework and chores, but I was so upset. He had
no right to ground me!" she screamed. Then she saw
the expression on her mother's face and froze.

"He does have the right to correct you. There are a
lot of things you can change about your life, but your
father isn't one of them. Like it or not you will always
be his daughter," Megan said, keeping her voice low
and even.

Jess looked at her, aghast.

"He is your father. And you owe him an apology,"
Megan said firmly.

"Do I have to?" Jess asked, horrified at the thought.

"How would you feel if he talked to you like that?

I know he hasn't been around for most of your life, but that doesn't excuse your behavior. I've taught you better than that," her mother reminded her.

"Am I grounded?" she wailed.

"Would I ground you if you had treated me like that?" Megan asked.

Jess gulped, then flung herself across the bed. "Nobody cares about me."

"You're wrong. We all love you, but you can't treat people any way you like. Your dad has made some mistakes, but he's human and he has feelings. You need to make amends. You were wrong to stay on the phone and you know it," Megan said quietly.

"I blamed him for something the other night. Later, I told him I was sorry and I felt a lot better," she admitted, knowing Jess had probably heard them arguing.

"Think it over, I'm not going to force you to apologize." Megan kissed the top of her daughter's head and closed the door as she left.

Mitchell was still sitting in silence when Megan came downstairs. She let him be and went to fix dinner.

A while later she heard the steps creak and knew Jess was coming downstairs. She resisted the urge to listen when Jess went to the family room.

Zack came in as Megan was putting dinner on the table. "Would you please go tell your dad and Jess, dinner is ready?"

Zack came back almost immediately. "Could you hold up for a few minutes? They both look kind of upset."

Megan nodded. She and Zack sat and talked while they waited. A short while later Mitchell and Jess came in the kitchen together.

While they were eating, the phone rang. Zack answered it. "Jess, are you going skating?" he asked. She shook her head sadly. He passed the message along.

After dinner Mitchell insisted on helping Jess with her homework. Grudgingly, she obeyed. As they worked together they found they had some mutual interest. They ended the evening by playing a game of Scrabble together.

Megan was folding clothes when Jess came to tell her good-night. "Is everything all right?" she asked.

Jess nodded, subdued. "He helped me with my homework...I apologized," she admitted reluctantly.

Megan smiled. "I'm proud of you. I know it was a hard thing to do, but I knew you would do what was right."

Jess shrugged. It hadn't been as bad as she expected. "You know what? He said he was sorry he missed me being a baby. He wants me to tell him all the stories about when I was little."

Megan put down her work and hugged her daughter tightly.

After ten o'clock Mitchell came hobbling into the kitchen. "Are you still working?" he asked, watching her fix lunches for the next day.

After she put the food in the refrigerator, she said, "I think I'll call it a night."

They climbed the stairs with their arms around one another, both relieved at the way the day had turned out. Outside the guest room, Megan asked, "Need any help?"

"You've already given me more than I deserve. Thank you," he said genuinely.

"'Night, Mitch,'' she said, feeling a little embarrassed, and hurried to her room.

Mitch stood in the hallway, thinking about the day.

Zack heard his mother in her bedroom. He wanted to talk to his father and find out what was going on. He found him standing in the hallway, staring at his mother's bedroom door. "Dad, is everything okay?"

Mitchell shuffled to the guest room, and Zack followed. "Jess and I had a clash today," he said wearily.

"Then I'm surprised you don't look worse," Zack said, chuckling.

"Your mother helped me," he explained, trying to take off his robe.

"What did you expect?" Zack asked, helping him.

"I don't know," he said. He felt bone tired. "Actually, I expected her to throw me out when she got home and found Jess upset. It's not like there wasn't enough going on yesterday!"

"You don't know Mom," Zack said. "She never lets us get away with anything. I got caught drinking when I was about thirteen. A bunch of boys were camping out in this kid's yard. One of the other guy's parents drank a lot. He figured they wouldn't miss a bottle. He brought it over in his sleeping bag. We were scared at first, then he dared us. After that it didn't take much to keep us going.

"Before the kid's dad went to bed, he checked on us. We were wasted. He hauled us in the house and called our parents.

"Mom showed up first. She thanked the man for calling. We rode home in silence," he said, sitting down on the bed near his father.

"I thought I was a big shot. She wasn't going to tell *me* what to do. I was taller, so I stood up to her and put on this macho act. I told her she'd embarrassed me in front of my friends, and to get off my case. I was really cocky. She reached up and caught my ear, pulling me down to her level. She told me we had a date the next night, and before I said another word I had better give it some serious thought. She really scared me.

"The next night Gran stayed with Jess, while Mom and I went out. Whew! First she took me to an Alcoholics Anonymous meeting. People stood up and told how drinking had ruined their lives and broken up their families. That kind of hit home—especially when one of the speakers was only a few years older than me. I thought about you a lot that night," Zack admitted.

"Then we drove through this place where people were hanging out on the street. It was pretty scary. After that, Mom drove me to the emergency room. Doc met us there. We sat in the waiting room, while he told me about alcoholism, alcohol poisoning and a few other things drinking can do to your body and brain," Zack said quietly.

"Well, anyway, you get the picture. Mom took me home after that. No lecture or yelling or grounding me. She'd made her point," said Zack thoughtfully. "That's one night I'll never forget!"

"You know why she did it, don't you? She didn't want you to turn out like me," Mitchell said, looking in his son's face.

"But you've changed," Zack said.

"Sometimes, even now, the desire to drink hits me really hard. Then I'm reminded of what I have to lose by doing that," Mitchell said seriously.

Zack was almost afraid to ask. "Are days like today hard?"

"Yep. It would be much easier to give in and get drunk than to try to work out all these problems. Much easier," Mitchell admitted. He and Zack lapsed into silence, both considering the consequences of an action like that.

"You know, I remember the day you left. I'd been staying with Gran, while Mom was in the hospital. We went to help you get the apartment cleaned up and ready for Mom. Only you weren't there. Gran sent me to my room to play. I heard Mom come in and ran to her. She hugged and kissed me. Then she asked where you were..." Zack's eyes teared up at the memory.

"What happened?" Mitchell not only wanted to know, he *needed* to know.

"Gran gave Mom a piece of paper. She read it, then screamed like I never heard a person scream before. Then she dropped to her knees, holding the note to her heart and crying. She kept saying she loved you." Tears trickled down Zack's face as he remembered his mother's agony.

"You never should have left her, Dad. She needed you," Zack finished in a choking voice. Then he walked out of the room without another word.

Chapter Ten

Each day as Mitchell improved, all the faces Megan loved looked at her with a question. What would she do? She wanted time, lots of time, to be sure she made the right decision. But time was running out and she was feeling pressured.

There were questions that needed asking. She feared the answers. With answers there would be decisions to make. Life would be forever altered according to those decisions. So she shrank away from it, letting fear hold her hostage.

After another late night of working around the house, Megan started for bed. She noticed the lamp was still on in the guest room and tiptoed in to turn it off. As she was leaving, Mitchell whispered, "Don't I get a kiss good-night?"

"Sorry, I didn't mean to wake you," she said very softly.

"I wasn't asleep."

"Anything wrong?"

"No. I was waiting for you to tuck me in and give me a kiss," he said, smiling.

She straightened the covers, fluffed the pillows and put an extra pillow under his arm. "How's that?"

"Great! Now the kiss." Megan kissed his cheek. "That's not what I had in mind," he teased.

Frustration engulfed her and she sat down on the bed next to him. "I can't."

"Why not?" he asked, watching her expression in the dim light.

"This isn't some game we're playing. This is for keeps."

"At this point, all I want is for you to kiss me goodnight. Is that too much to ask?" he persisted.

"I'm afraid," she whimpered, studying his face in the shadowy light. He was very appealing to her. She gently stroked his cheek with the back of her hand. "You want so much," she said quietly, knowing the future was on their minds, that this pretense was only a way to bring the subject to the surface.

"True. I want you to love me the way you used to."

His voice was so quiet that Megan had to strain to hear each word. Her head sank to her chest. She wasn't ready to acknowledge that she wanted the same thing. He lightly put his hand on her neck and gently urged her toward him. Nose to nose in the still of the night, he spoke words she wasn't ready to deal with. "I want you back," he murmured.

She placed her cheek next to his. He could feel the hot tears running from her face to his. He patted her back softly. "What can I do to make things easier for you?"

"Nothing," she cried.

"If I could go back and do it all over again, I would," he assured her.

"That's just it, Mitch, you can't. You made other things more important to you than me." She sniffed, her heart was aching.

"I never set out for things to turn out this way. Meg, I love you so much."

He sounded so sincere. Megan wanted to ask the question that was on her mind, but the words stuck in her throat. She sat up and wiped her eyes on the edge of the sheet.

"Come on, give me a kiss good-night." He smiled warmly and nudged her to him. She kissed him quickly, then rushed out.

Mitchell was encouraged. He fell asleep filled with hope.

Megan went to her room and wrestled with her fears and misgivings most of the night.

The next morning Megan left the house before having to face anyone. At work, Ted immediately asked if she was all right. She knew her feelings must be showing. "Not you too!" she roared.

"Come on, this isn't like you. What's the problem? You look like you could fly apart. I'm concerned about you," he said soothingly.

"I'm sorry, I didn't mean to take it out on you. I need some answers," she admitted to her old friend.

"Have you asked the questions?"

"No. I'm afraid," she moaned.

"Nothing will be settled until you do," Ted told her. He figured this had to do with Mitchell. "You can't run away from him forever."

Megan nodded, knowing he had given her the solution. But she still wasn't sure she wanted to confront the particulars of Mitchell's past.

At lunch time she asked Ted to watch things while she went home for a few minutes. When she came into the house, Ruth could feel the tension between her son and his wife. "Megan, I'm glad you're home. I need to run out and pick something up. Here, eat this sandwich while you're here," she said, and made a hasty exit.

Alone, Mitchell and Megan sat at the table eating their lunch in strained silence. Finally, Mitchell reached over and took Megan's hand. "What's wrong?" he asked, concerned.

"I don't know you. You've been places, seen things, done things I know nothing about. You look like Mitch, but you're not the same man who left here," she said, shocked at her own words.

"No, I'm not the same," he agreed. "I never want to be that man again."

"But I loved him!"

"He was a drunk. He made you miserable—or have you forgotten?" He confidently dismissed the man from his past, casting him aside as though he no longer existed.

Megan needed to get away, her heart was racing. "I better go."

"When are you going to stop running away from me?"

"I'm not running. I have a business to get back to," she said, jumping up and clearing the table. Then she bolted for the door.

Mitchell stood up. "Every time I try to get close to you, you run or push me away. What are you afraid of, Megan?"

Megan stopped and looked back, staring at him impatiently, feeling trapped. "I'm not running, Mitchell. What do you want?"

"You won't even give me a decent kiss, much less a chance to prove myself," he accused, knowing that, cornered and challenged, she would react.

She got a determined look on her face, marched over to him, reached up on her tiptoes, and gave him a firm kiss. "Decent?" she asked fuming.

He didn't even have to answer; his eyes said no.

Megan decided she would give him that decent kiss he wanted so much, no matter how she felt. She flung her arms roughly around his neck and was about to give him a hard, uncaring kiss. Then she stopped short.

Mitchell's eyes were twinkling. She realized that only a man who really knew her could have maneuvered her into this position. She reached up and kissed him tenderly, then dropped back, shaken.

Mitchell bent slightly, watching to see if she was going to bolt. When she didn't, he slowly gathered her to him and kissed her the way he had been wanting to for a long time.

For a few seconds Megan was speechless. "I...I'd better go. Ted has a landscape job this afternoon," she explained and hurried out. On the way back to work, she reprimanded herself for letting her emotions carry her away.

Megan was distracted all afternoon. Everything felt as if it was pushing in on her. As she was closing the shop, she suddenly remembered something else she needed to do, and sent her son home without her.

At the kitchen window, getting a drink of water, Zack caught sight of his mother hurriedly walking toward the river. He was sure something was bothering her.

Zack took the initiative and put dinner on the table, figuring his mother would be gone for a while. When Mitch asked her whereabouts, Zack repeated what she had told him. After dinner he hovered in the kitchen, keeping watch for her.

Mitchell came to the kitchen after Jess went to bed. He glanced out the kitchen door. "What did you say your mother had to do?" he asked, noticing that the truck and van were both parked outside, and that the shop was dark.

"She didn't tell me," he said, looking out the window for the twentieth time.

"Where is she?" Mitchell asked, turning to Zack.

His son looked away, realizing he should have said something before. "She wasn't herself. I saw her heading up there." He nodded in the direction of The Hill.

"Why didn't you say something sooner?" Mitchell's voice rose. "It's dark out. Did she have a light?"

"She only goes up there when she needs to get away and think. I thought she'd be back long before now," Zack explained.

They got in the truck and took off down the road. With flashlights in hand, they started scrambling up the path. Near the top they both stopped. They could hear her sobbing in the distance.

"Why don't you wait here? I have a feeling I need to talk to her alone," Mitchell told his son.

His head was throbbing and his heart was racing as he followed the mournful sound. Finding her sitting on the rock, he called her name softly. "Meg?"

She jumped with fright. "What are you doing up here?" she asked between sobs.

"I came to get you," he said, holding out his hand to her.

"I...ca-can't...stop crying."

Mitchell gently caught her arm and pulled her toward him. She slid off the rock and into his arms. Great heaving sobs erupted. He held her close, letting her cry. When it seemed she wouldn't stop, he decided they had to talk regardless. Reluctantly he asked, "What's the cause of all this?"

"I feel like my heart is breaking. You told me I haven't forgiven you—it's true. I don't know if I can. I have to know..." she said, sobbing into his chest.

"Ask. Let's put the past to rest here and now." He had always known this day would come and he had dreaded it.

"I don't want to hear the answer. I don't want to know the truth," she cried, clinging to him.

Mitchell tried to comfort her. It wasn't possible. He decided to just get it over with. Prolonging this was only making matters worse. "Meg, I love you, only you. I've never loved anyone else." He stopped for a moment, hoping she'd heard him.

He knew he could lie to her, tell her what she wanted to hear. If he did, they would never stand a chance. As he allowed God to lead him, it had always been to the truth. To lie, at this point, would only be to get what he wanted. He knew if he did that now, sooner or later he would be making more and more trade-offs. It wouldn't take long to fall again. Not long at all.

He held her tight as he started speaking. "While I was away, I went all the way to the bottom. On my downward spiral I broke every commandment, but one..." Tears began choking his voice as he spoke. "I never killed anyone."

Megan tried to pull away. He held her more tightly, even though the struggle hurt his wounded body. "Listen to me. Please, just listen to me for a minute."

She stopped struggling and froze. "When I finally hit bottom, I wanted to die. I just wanted to die and get it over with. I had let everyone I cared about down, including myself. Most of all...you," he said shuddering, feeling if he let her go now, he would shatter into a million pieces.

"An old man found me in the gutter half-frozen one night. You don't know how many times I wished he had just left me there. I was out cold, I wouldn't have felt anything. But he carried me home with him and took care of me. I didn't ask for his help or his mercy, but he gave it anyway. I was out of my head. I had frostbite on my hands, feet and face. I didn't care. He nursed me back from death's door. I don't know why *he* thought I was worth saving—I didn't." Mitchell stopped for a moment, grieving to the depths of his soul.

"When I was finally conscious, he asked if he could call someone, family, someone who loved me. All I could see was your face. I wanted to see you so bad, but I knew it would be a mistake to call you. My life was in ruins. I remembered what you had told me, but you had added one stipulation. Don't break our marriage vows. If I did, you told me to never come back. Now I knew I couldn't come back...ever.

"That old man helped me get clean. I stayed with him for a long time trying to put my life back together. But there was always something missing. I had this empty ache inside. Part of me was missing...you. I fought it for years. I knew what you had told me and I knew you meant it. I figured you were better off without me anyway.'' He fought the turmoil that was raging inside him.

''I know I broke our wedding vows. I'm so sorry, Meg. If you could find it in your heart to forgive me…we could put our lives back together, the way they belong. Life will never be right unless we're together. The way God intended us to be. Please, Meg, forgive me,'' he begged.

Megan's worst fear had come to pass. Mitchell had been unfaithful. She believed there had to be faithfulness in a marriage for it to work. All those years of waiting for him, all those dreams of being together again, had just been destroyed. All at once she couldn't take any more. She went limp and dropped to the ground in a heap.

Mitchell yelled for Zack to help him. He was trying to revive Megan, when Zack came rushing up. ''What happened?''

''Let's get her back to the house,'' Mitchell said hoarsely.

Zack lifted his mother from the ground. Mitchell held the flashlight on the path so Zack could plan his steps down the steep hillside. Mitchell slipped and fell a couple of times on the way down. By the time Zack got his parents to the truck, he wasn't sure which one was in worse condition.

Back at the house, Zack gently laid his mother on her bed. Her eyes were open, but she was blankly staring, not speaking. Zack covered her, knowing she was in shock.

He rushed downstairs and found his father still standing where he had left him. ''Dad, what happened?''

Mitchell looked at him, but didn't really see him. "She doesn't want me back."

"Dad, she's upset. She's not herself," he said, trying to salvage his family.

"No. I've hurt her too badly. She'll never forgive me!"

Zack knew his father was in some kind of shock, too. He quickly dialed Doc. When he turned around, his father was gone. Zack found him in the guest room, packing. "Dad, what are you doing?" he asked, dismayed.

"I'm leaving. Your mother doesn't want me here," he admitted sadly.

"Dad, she's in shock. Don't leave us again," Zack begged.

"It was a mistake to move here. I'll just go over and stay with Gran," he said, trying to alleviate Zack's fears.

"I don't care about the past. I want you here," Zack cried. "I've prayed for ten years for you to come home. Don't you leave me again."

Mitchell put his arms around his son. "I love you, Zack, but I have to do what's best for your mom right now."

Doc came hurrying up the stairs. He caught the tail end of what Mitchell was saying. "What on earth is going on here?" he growled.

"I don't know. Mom went up on The Hill. It got late. Dad and I went up after her. She was all upset. Then she sort of fainted. She's out of her head, and Dad's packing to leave," Zack spewed out.

"Go fix me some coffee, Zack," Doc ordered. "I'll take care of things up here."

Zack went to the kitchen and dropped into one of the chairs.

Doc looked at the open suitcase. "Mitchell, what do you think you're doing?"

"I'm moving to Mom's. I should have done that in the first place. Megan didn't need all this dumped on her."

"What happened?" Doc asked calmly.

"Doc, this is between Meg and me, nobody else," Mitchell said.

Doc sat him on the bed, looking at his cuts and scrapes. "Let me clean those up," he said, starting to work on the injuries. "Nothing is that simple. The kids need you. So does Megan. I know you two can work it out—if you try."

"I know you mean well, but just stay out of this," Mitchell insisted.

"You looking for an excuse to pick up the old life-style, Mitchell?" Doc asked, knowing that would get the man thinking. Mitchell refused to answer.

Doc finished patching him up and went to check on Megan. She looked like she must have had a pretty good cry. She was balled up, staring into space. Doc sat down on the bed beside her. "Megan, what's wrong?" he asked, patting her back.

She didn't acknowledge his presence. "Megan, Mitchell is packing to move out. Is that what you want?" She didn't answer, but he noticed her eyes were welling up.

"Is there anything I can do?" he asked. She shook her head. "I'll call you tomorrow," he said, patting her again, feeling like crying himself.

Doc returned to the guest room. "Mitchell, did it

ever occur to you that despite what happened between the two of you, maybe she needs for you to stay.''

Mitchell gave him a hard look. ''I'm the reason she's like that—and you think I should stay?''

''Maybe I'm wrong, but do you think it's right for you to just pack up and run out? You did that once before. I was with her. I saw how devastated she was then.'' Doc drove his point home. ''Is that what you want to do again?''

''No,'' Mitch said quietly, remembering Zack's description of her reaction. ''What should I do?''

''I'm going to give you some advice, which I rarely do. You go downstairs and reassure Zack he isn't going to be fatherless again. Then send him to bed. After that you try to talk to Megan. She wants to crawl in a hole right now and close it behind her, but don't let her. Tell her how you feel, whether she wants to hear it or not. If she won't talk to you, get some rest. Don't make any decisions until tomorrow, okay?'' Doc said.

Mitchell heard him out and knew he was right. They went downstairs and found Zack crumpled at the table. ''Zack, I'm not going anywhere tonight. I'm sorry about before. Go on to bed. We'll figure this out tomorrow,'' he said, squeezing his son's shoulder. ''No matter what happens, son, I won't leave you again.''

''What about Mom?'' Zack wanted to be reassured that she would be all right.

''I'll see to her. You go on to bed,'' he said, letting his son know he was back in control of himself.

Zack went upstairs and glanced in his mother's room. Her back was to him. He didn't know what to say to her, so he went to his room.

Mitchell fixed a cup of tea and took it up to Megan, setting it on the nightstand. She was facing the wall, staring blankly. He came around the bed and knelt in front of her. She closed her eyes, shutting him out. He couldn't blame her. "Meg…I'm sorry. I had to tell you the truth. Neither one of us could live with this lie between us. I know I've messed up everything. I don't deserve another chance, but I'm asking for one anyway. I love you," he said, leaning over and lightly kissing her cheek.

Megan covered her face and began to sob. Mitchell felt totally inadequate. For him to keep saying he was sorry didn't make a bit of difference. The damage was done. He wished he could take it all back. He slipped off her shoes and tucked her into bed, deciding the best thing he could do, at the moment, was to let her be.

In the guest room, he lay on the bed, staring at the ceiling the rest of the night, hating himself.

Early in the morning he heard Megan's shower start. He felt awful in every way possible. He went to fix breakfast, hoping for a chance to talk to her.

Megan came downstairs ready for work. "I fixed you some breakfast," Mitchell said, hoping she would listen to him.

"Thanks, but I'm not really hungry," she said, still close to tears.

"At least have some coffee. You haven't had anything since lunch yesterday," he reminded her with concern in his voice. Lunch yesterday—that seemed like a million years ago.

"Sit down for a minute, please," he requested quietly. Megan eased into a chair as he put a cup of coffee in front of her. "Last night was a nightmare. Meg, I can't say anything that will change the facts. I truly wish I could. I would do anything to make this easier for you," he said sincerely.

When she didn't respond, he asked, "Would it be better for you if I went to stay with Mom?"

Megan glanced at him. He was pale, scraped up, and looked like he hadn't gotten much sleep either. Tears began to trickle down her face. She nodded, seeing a likeness to her own suffering in his eyes. Jumping up, she dashed out the kitchen door.

A few seconds later Zack came in the kitchen. "I heard you talking, but I didn't hear her answer," he admitted.

"I'm moving to Gran's this morning," he said solemnly.

"I don't want you to leave. Doesn't that count for anything?"

"It does, but this is your mother's house. She's not comfortable with me here. Believe me, she has good reasons, so don't take this out on her."

Zack sighed in resignation. Neither felt like eating, so they went up and started packing Mitchell's belongings.

They were carrying boxes out when Jess came out of her room, rubbing her eyes. "What's going on?" she asked when she saw the boxes.

"I'm much better, so I'm going to stay with your grandmother for a while," Mitchell said, trying to sound cheerful.

"But I don't want you to go," Jess said, shocking her father and herself.

Mitchell sat on the bed and patted the place beside him. Jess plopped down with her arms folded, pouting. "Jess, we'll go out like we did before and you can come to Gran's anytime you like."

"It's not the same. You won't be here to help me with my homework and stuff. Nobody else wants to play games with me. Please don't go, Daddy," she cried.

Mitchell hugged her tightly. She had finally called him *Daddy* and he was on the way out the door again. He couldn't do anything right. His heart felt so heavy that he didn't know how he would go on.

"Are you and Mom getting a divorce?" Jess wailed as the thought hit her.

"No, don't you worry about that. This doesn't have anything to do with you or Zack. It's just between your mom and me," he tried to reassure her. "I hurt your mother's feelings very badly a long time ago. She was kind enough to let me stay here while I was getting well. I'm much better, so it's time for me to go."

"When you and I got mad you didn't leave," she pointed out.

"Why don't you get dressed and give us a hand? We'll ride over to Gran's and you can spend the day with me, okay?" he said. There was no way he could explain the situation to his daughter.

Mitchell stared straight ahead as they drove past the flower shop. He didn't want to know if Megan was watching or not.

Megan was watching from the window when the truck drove away with Zack, Jess and Mitchell in it. Her heart broke all over again.

Ruth answered the door and accepted her son without question.

No mention of Mitchell moving out was made when Zack arrived at work. He told his mother that Jess was with her grandmother and that he would pick her up later. After that he kept his distance and his thoughts to himself.

After work, Zack went to pick up Jess but only stayed a few minutes. He was having trouble believing that they could do this.

Megan entered the empty house, fixed herself a cup of tea and carried it upstairs. She tried to avoid the guest room, but she was drawn to look inside. All signs of Mitchell had been removed.

She felt as empty as the room looked. Wasn't once enough? She had let him hurt her twice. He had betrayed her and their marriage. She would never be able to pretend it hadn't happened or that it didn't matter. It did.

Megan needed to be comforted, but there was no one there for her. The hopes and dreams she had secretly held on to for years were now empty illusions.

Chapter Eleven

Megan had been having a mental battle with herself all day. Things were either right or wrong. The rules were made a long time ago, and you weren't supposed to break them. She put a fresh cup of tea beside the one she hadn't touched the night before. She didn't want to think about it anymore. She lay across the bed, trying to forget Mitchell's confession.

Early evening the children returned home and Jess immediately came charging into her mother's room. "Why did Daddy have to leave?" she demanded.

"He only came here to recover," Megan said, trying to sound convincing.

"Don't you love him anymore?" Zack asked, wanting deeper answers.

"It's better this way," Megan replied.

"Better for who? It's sure not better for Jess or me. Both of you are miserable. Gran's upset. So who is it better for, Mom?" Zack cried out.

Megan didn't have an answer for him. The broken vows were between her and Mitchell, no one else.

"Okay, I know Dad messed up a long time ago, but he's changed. Doesn't he deserve a second chance?" Zack insisted.

"This is between your father and me!" Megan said, putting a stop to the questions.

"Fine, if that's the way you want it," Zack said, perturbed. "Jess and I have plans tonight. Do you want us to cancel and stay home with you?"

Megan shook her head. Both walked out, leaving her alone. The very thing she had been trying to avoid was happening: everyone was hurt.

A little later, Doc came roaring in. Megan suspected Zack had called him again. "Well, I hope you and Mitchell are satisfied. I thought you might be interested in knowing he's back in bed. That little mountain climb last night did it."

"Will he be okay?" Megan asked meekly, feeling responsible for his condition.

"He will, if he'll take care of himself! If you two can't work out your personal problems. Think of how this is affecting the kids," he grumbled.

"Look, you're the one who asked me to bring him home," she snapped.

"And you're the one who made the decision to do so. Why did you do it?" he asked calmly, knowing he had given her something to think about. She peered at him, waiting for him to make his point. "I just gave you a little push. I didn't make you do anything you didn't want to do. I'm not defending his past actions, he's been a first-class jerk. But Megan, I really believe he's changed. I know he's hurt you deeply, but I also know the man loves you."

Megan turned away. Doc grabbed her arm and turned her back. "Now you listen to me. If you think

I'm going to let you crawl in a hole of self-pity, forget it. Those kids need you. So get up and go fix them dinner. Me, too!'' he ordered.

She glared at him, then her face crumpled. "It hurts so much," she cried.

"I know," he said, putting his arms around her.

"I'm so tired of fighting all this. I don't think the nightmare will ever end."

Doc patted her like a child. "We all feel like that sometimes, but you can't give up," he reminded her. "God will give you the strength to get through this, just like He has all the other hard times in your life."

Megan nodded and wiped her eyes, surprised at his mention of God. Last she heard, Doc wasn't on speaking terms with Him.

"Come on, I'm starving," he said, dragging her from the room.

They were eating dinner when the phone rang. Zack answered it. "Mom, it's Gran. She wants to know if you'll talk to her," he said, holding out the phone.

Megan gave him a look that said "Don't be absurd," and took the phone from him. "Why would I not talk to you?" she asked Ruth.

"I didn't know how you were feeling. Are you okay?" she asked, concerned.

"So-so, Doc is over here harassing me." She sighed.

"Then you're in good hands. I would have come over, but I've been kind of busy," she apologized, sounding disheartened.

"How is he?" Megan asked quietly, noticing everyone was listening. She pulled the phone cord as far as it would stretch and went into the hall for a little privacy.

"I'm worried about him. He doesn't want to eat, he

just stares at nothing. I don't know what to do," Ruth admitted.

"Tell him I said—"

Ruth stopped her. "I'm sorry, Megan, but I'm not going to pass messages for either one of you. I love you both. Please don't put me in the middle," Ruth said shakily.

Megan hesitated a moment. "Let me talk to him." There was a long silence before she heard the extension being picked up.

"Hello," Mitchell said tonelessly.

"Mitchell, it's Megan," she said softly.

"Meg!" His voice registered his surprise.

"Why aren't you taking care of yourself?" she asked, hurrying on.

"Does it matter to you?" he said listlessly.

"Yes."

He felt a glimmer of hope. "Could we get together and talk sometime?"

"I don't think that's a good idea right now. You need to take care of yourself and get back on your feet. Doc says you don't need any more stress," she said unsteadily.

"Will you still let me see the kids?" he asked, needing something to hold on to.

"Yes." She paused a moment. "They can come over there."

"Are you glad I'm gone?" he asked, wanting to know.

Megan's heart ached. "I can't talk about this now."

"What can I say or do?" he pleaded.

"I think we said all there is to say." She was shaking uncontrollably.

"You don't love me anymore—do you? Do you want a…'' He couldn't say it.

"God help us!" she said so quietly that he barely heard her. Then she dropped the phone and ran up to her room in tears.

There was nothing to do but go on. Each person had to fill the void in their heart their own way.

Megan saw Cass at church shortly thereafter. She approached Megan looking a bit subdued. "How's Mitchell?" she asked.

"He's improving," Megan said, passing on what Ruth had told her.

"Could I come by and see him?" her sister asked timidly.

Megan looked at her sister, shocked. She decided she may as well tell her, even though she would say "I told you so." "He's doing much better, so he moved in with Ruth."

Now it was Cass's turn to look stunned. She didn't say anything else.

Reverend Goodwin spoke to Megan after church. "How are things at home?"

"Getting back to normal," she said, trying to sound cheerful. "Mitchell moved to his mother's house a few days ago."

"You don't look very happy about it," he observed.

"Things will eventually turn out for the best," she said positively.

"I'll keep your family in my prayers," he said kindly.

"Thank you. We appreciate that," Megan said moving on.

After church, the kids went over to see their father.

Alone again, Megan spent the afternoon walking around the farm. She had no desire to go to The Hill, it now held unpleasant memories. She settled by the river bank and let her thoughts wander.

She'd kept her life on hold long enough waiting for Mitch. But where would she go from here? Broken vows and promises surrounded her. Maybe it was time to make some changes. She needed something to look forward to. Her eyes scanned the empty field beside the river.

Megan got up as her mind began to twirl. She had always intended to do something with that field. It would be a wonderful place to build a landscape garden. She looked at it from all angles. She could see a gazebo, a rock garden with a waterfall and a trellis. Water would be no problem. The idea quickly took form, and she decided to start on it the next day.

The following morning, Megan told Ted her plans for the garden. He was surprised when she asked him to handle the business that afternoon. She explained that she was planning to do most of the project herself.

She went to the local building supply store and made some purchases. When the lumber and supplies were delivered, Megan dug in like a groundhog. The blueprint was in her head, so she worked alone until dark.

As the garden progressed, she let a lot of the housework slide, and most nights dinner was frozen food. The kids didn't complain; instead they came out and gave her a hand on the nights they weren't with their dad. At bedtime Megan would fall asleep from exhaustion.

When the Junior Prom rolled around, Mitchell let Zack drive his car. His date's parents were divorced, so they had to visit four houses. By the time they got to the dance, neither was in much of a party mood. They went to the after-prom party and stayed out all night, just to say they had done so.

Jess went back and forth between her parents without much complaint. Megan even let her spend a weekend with Mitchell.

As Mitchell regained his strength, he took the children out to eat and found all sorts of things to entertain them. Both parents avoided the subject of the other, so there was often little to talk about.

As Megan's project took shape, the same guy delivered the order every time. He began to hang around and talk to her. It bothered her that he was being paid to work and was goofing off. Then she discovered he owned the company and liked getting to know his customers.

Mike Sutton had also built his own business. He had two children and was divorced. He found Megan bright and attractive, even under the layers of dirt that usually covered her.

Meanwhile, through the children, Megan heard Mitchell was back at his job. Ruth called once in a while, but their conversations were strained.

Just when things were beginning settle down a little, Mitchell called Zack close to eleven one evening. Megan overheard her son saying he would be right there.

"You aren't going out now," she said firmly, trying to stop him.

"Yes, I am. Dad needs me to help him," he said impatiently. When he saw she wasn't moved, he turned to leave without her permission.

"Where are you going?" she demanded.

"To help a friend in trouble," he said.

"No! The last time your father did something like this he wound up in the hospital. You're not going!" she yelled.

"Yes, I am," he shouted and stalked out.

It was late in the night before Zack returned. Megan heard him come in, but she didn't get up. She knew in this angry state, she was bound to say the wrong thing.

The next morning, Zack tried to justify his actions at breakfast. "Mom, I wasn't in any danger. I was at the hospital. Someone I know tried to kill himself. He doesn't want anyone to know about it. That's why I didn't tell you," he explained.

"Is he all right?" Megan asked concerned.

"He will be. Dad was great. He knew just the right things to say. He must have lived through a lot we don't know about," he said, hoping she would be interested in hearing more about his father.

"I'm really sorry about your friend. But don't ever do that to me again!"

"Don't do what? Go help a friend in trouble? Isn't that what you always taught us to do, help our fellow man. Or does it only apply when Dad isn't involved?" When his mother didn't answer, he continued. "You know I can make some decisions for myself!"

"Well, if you decide to make some of your father's old decisions, you won't be making them here," she said sharply, glaring at him. They had always been close, and he had always been obedient. Now it seemed every time they had a disagreement, it involved Mitchell.

"You know, Mom, you're a hypocrite. You say to do things one way, while you do them another. Don't tell me what to do, if you aren't willing to do as you say. You say to forgive others. Mom, you need to forgive Dad!'' Zack said, then walked out.

Megan was crushed. Zack had never talked to her like that before. The security she thought she had in her family seemed to have cracks. She was trying to be a good Christian. Why was she the one who was always wrong?

She threw herself into her project. Mike kept stopping by, and they talked about the problems of being single parents. He seemed to be the only person she could talk to right now. With everyone else, she always seemed to be defending herself.

School let out for the summer, and Mitchell sent word through Zack that he wanted to take all of them to the beach for a week.

''Mom, please go with us,'' Zack begged.

''I can't, I have too much work to do,'' she said, using her same old excuse.

The kids packed up and went without her.

Alone, Megan worked nonstop. Ted sent one of the men to help when the gazebo was delivered. The temperature was well over ninety degrees. Mike stuck around to give them a hand, seeming to be in no hurry.

''Where's Zack? I haven't seen him around,'' Mike asked curiously.

''He and Jess went to the beach with their father,'' she said.

Later that evening Mike showed up. ''Are you still working? I came by your house, but nobody was there,'' he said, walking over to where she was spreading mulch around newly planted shrubs.

Megan looked around, startled. ''I didn't expect to

see you again today," she said, wondering why he was there.

"I thought I'd come by for a visit. I figured you might be lonely with everyone out of town. I brought you some dinner," he said, holding up a pizza.

Unable to think of a reason to refuse, she led him into the gazebo, and they sat down. "Why are you making these improvements?" he asked to put her at ease.

"People like to see what they're getting. If they can get an idea of how landscaping can improve the looks of their property, they're more likely to buy." Once she'd explained her marketing strategy, he understood how she'd managed to build herself such a nice little business. They chatted for almost an hour.

As Megan collected the trash, she realized how tired she was. "Well, this was really nice, Mike, but I need to get home."

"You look beat, I'll give you a ride, since it's right on my way," he said, grinning.

She dusted herself off before she dared get in his expensive car. On the short ride to the house, she decided to ask him a question that had been on her mind. "If you don't mind my asking, why did you and your wife get a divorce?"

"She was busy with the kids and the house. I felt last on her list. I had an affair. She found out and divorced me," he admitted, as they stopped near the house.

"Thanks for dinner," Megan said, hurriedly getting out.

Mike hopped out of the car as well. "Wait a minute," he called. Megan stopped. "Look I know I sound glib about all this, but really I'm not. I made a terrible mistake. I tried to straighten things out with my wife. She just couldn't forgive me. I regret it more now than I did at the time it happened.''

He stared at her with a deep sadness in his eyes, hoping she'd understand. Suddenly his whole story came pouring out. Megan actually felt sorry for him after he finished telling her all his woes.

''I came by because I'm lonely. I can talk to you. You understand,'' he said.

''I'm sorry, Mike. The breakup of any marriage is sad, especially when there are children involved. They're the innocent victims who get hurt,'' she replied.

''That's true. My kids are confused and mad at both of us. We're pulling them back and forth, and it's not right,'' he said downhearted. ''What about you? What's the deal with you and your husband? You never say much about him.''

Megan sighed heavily. ''Maybe another time. I'm just too tired right now. Thanks again for bringing dinner,'' she said, starting for the house.

''How about Friday night? I'll take you out to dinner and you can tell me your story. You need to get away from work for a while,'' he called after her.

Megan turned to look at him. She smiled warmly, then shook her head. ''Thanks,'' she said, and sauntered to the house.

By late Friday morning the landscape garden was completed. Megan led Ted out to do a final inspection. ''This looks great. You outdid yourself, Megan,'' he said, patting her on the back.

''So what do I do with myself now that it's finished?'' she asked, fatigued.

Ted was expecting her to be overjoyed that the job

was done. Instead, she was back at loose ends. He knew she needed a break. "Why don't you join the kids at the beach and relax for the weekend?" he suggested. "I can manage things here tomorrow."

"I'll think about it," she said, giving him the keys to the van. "I'll take tomorrow off anyway. Thanks."

Mitchell tried to call Megan that night. He called again the next day without getting an answer. He tried again and again. Finally he called Ted at home.

"I'm sorry, Mitch, I don't know. She took the day off. I thought maybe she'd joined you guys. Is there anything I can do?" Ted asked, sensing he was concerned.

"No, that's okay. I just thought you might know where she was," Mitchell said.

After promising the kids they could spend the last day on the beach, Mitchell wasn't about to disappoint them, although he was ready to leave. Of course the day crawled by at a snail's pace.

Sunday night when they pulled in the driveway of the farmhouse the lights were on. Mitchell leaped out of the car and rushed inside before anyone else. He skidded to a halt when he found Megan sitting at the kitchen table sipping tea. "Where have you been the last two days?" he roared.

"I've been right here," she said calmly.

"I tried to call. You never answered," he griped.

"I was outside most of the time. Is something wrong?"

"I called Ted. He said he thought you were joining us. Where were you?"

At last Megan understood. "You thought I'd taken off," she laughed. It was the first time she had seen him since the day he moved out. He was tanned and looking very good, even though he was boiling mad.

"I was painting the side of the house. I used the truck to brace the ladder."

He went pale. "You were up on a ladder and no one knew!"

"It's no big deal. I've done it before," she said, brushing him off.

Just then the kids came in hauling their stuff. At the same time, he noticed that she didn't have on her rings. He didn't want to continue the discussion in front of them, so he waited.

Megan gave Zack and Jess a big hug. "I missed you guys so much. Did you have a good time?" They both grinned. She could tell they were worn-out. "Put your dirty clothes by the washer and get your stuff unpacked before you conk out."

Both dumped most of what they were carrying on the floor in the laundry room. Jess fished a shell necklace out of her pocket and latched it around her mother's neck. "I love it!" Megan said excitedly.

Zack brought in a huge box and stood it in front of her. She read the outside and started laughing. "A hammock!"

"I bought some extra rope, too. I plan to tie you in it and make you take it easy," he teased. She gave him a big hug.

"I'll use it, I promise. As soon as I finish painting the house."

"So that's where you were," Zack said. "I tried to call you a couple of times. I figured you were still working on the garden."

Megan glanced over at Mitchell. "You should have

told your father. He thought I had run off." Mitchell scowled angrily at her.

Ruth came dragging in with the last of the rubble. "Hi, Megan," she said, grinning wearily. "We had a wonderful time. I don't think I could stand much more fun."

Megan gave her a warm hug. "You look great. You all do. You must have had a good time," she said, pleased.

They all agreed it had been a lot of fun. The kids thanked their father and grandmother and headed for their rooms.

"Thanks for letting them go with us. The only thing that would have made it better was if you had gone, too," Ruth said, looking ready to collapse. "I'm beat. I'll wait for you in the car," she told her son.

"I'll be right with you," Mitchell said.

Megan turned to face Mitch. She knew he had something to say to her. All the peace and calm that had been on her face was now gone.

"Where were you last night? I called until about one," he said steadily.

"I had a date. We went out dancing. It was wonderful," she replied breezily, knowing she was goading him.

"Is that why you took your rings off?" he snarled.

Megan looked down at her paint-stained hand. "Of course, you didn't expect me to wear them on a date, did you?" she asked, leveling her look at him.

"You should have let me know where you were," he said, his jaw tightening visibly. "The kids could have needed you."

"Did you ever think of that while *you* were gone? I was out for a few hours," she said, stressing her point.

"What is this? A vendetta?"

She chose not to respond.

"Don't do this, Megan. You'll be sorry," he said, suddenly contrite.

"I haven't done anything and I'm already sorry! Sorry I put my life on hold waiting for you. So you could show up and tell me…" She looked away, overwhelmed. "Everything isn't about you, Mitchell. I needed to get out and have a little fun. When a friend asked, I accepted," she said hotly.

"What have you done?" he asked, trying to control his fear and anger.

"Nothing!" she sneered at him.

He came over and held her shoulders. "Then why did you feel the need to take off your rings?"

"Because they were dirty," she said, keeping her voice even.

"You told me you'd never taken them off before."

She searched his eyes. "I hadn't."

"Did you want to see how it felt?"

"Maybe."

"Are you thinking about getting a divorce?" he asked through gritted teeth.

"I've been thinking about a lot of things lately," she said, her anger matching his. "I've been wondering what I was waiting for!"

All at once he softened. "Please, Meg, don't do something stupid like I did. Don't give up on us," he begged.

"It's very revealing to see how little faith you have in me," she said calmly.

Mitchell let his hands drop from her shoulders to her hands. He felt her finger for the "groove." He was slightly reassured when he felt it. "'Let no man put asunder what God has joined together,'" he quoted.

Megan stared into his eyes as a lump formed in her throat. She pulled her hands free. "It's a shame you didn't remember those words," she said bitterly.

Mitchell stormed out of the house and got in his car. "She's taken her wedding ring off," he raged.

"Are you giving up?" Ruth asked calmly, irritating him further.

He started the car and drove away without answering—not wanting to tell his mother that Megan had had a date while they were gone.

Megan calmly went to the sink and picked up her rings from the window sill, scrubbing off the paint she had spilled on them. After she finished, she slipped them back on and went to hear about the trip.

All Jess could talk about was daddy. Megan finally tucked her in and kissed her good-night.

Then she went to Zack's room. "I heard you and Dad arguing. Did you make up?" he asked immediately.

"No. He doesn't approve of anything I did while you were away."

"He misses you. He was hoping you'd come to the beach for a couple of days."

"Maybe we'll go back before the summer is over or take a trip to the lake," she said, not wanting to argue anymore.

"All of us?" Zack asked hopefully.

Megan avoided answering him. "I'm tired, we'll talk in the morning. I missed you. Get a good night's sleep."

Zack gave up. His mother looked worn-out, and he was tired himself. He didn't want to start a fight with her. "I missed you, too. Good night, Mom."

Chapter Twelve

Since working herself to exhaustion had worked so far, Megan saw no reason to change tactics. Ted was doing fine without her, and she decided to take the afternoons off until the house painting was completed.

The next evening she was painting the eaves when she heard Mitchell angrily shout her name from the bottom of the ladder.

"What are you doing up there?" he yelled.

"Painting! I've done this before, I know what I'm doing," she said stubbornly.

"Why are you so mulish? You could get hurt!"

Finally she looked down at him. "Is there something I can help you with?"

"I came by to tell you I didn't mean to upset you the other evening."

"I wasn't upset. You were!"

"Yeah, I guess I was," he admitted. "I'm not leaving until you get off that ladder."

"Suit yourself," she said, continuing to paint.

"Got another brush?" he said, rolling up his sleeves.

A few minutes later he was painting. He tried to think of something to say that wouldn't start an argument. "I had a checkup with Doc the other day. You know what he told me? He went out on a date not long ago! I couldn't believe it," he said, astonished.

Megan accidentally slapped the paintbrush across her hand. She mumbled to herself as she pulled a rag out of her pocket and tried to wipe it off.

"It shocked me. It was like Mom telling me she had a date," Mitchell continued, not noticing her predicament.

"I'm sure he gets lonely. What did he say about your checkup?"

"Nothing much," he said, glancing to see if she was wearing her rings. He couldn't tell—she was rubbing her hand with a rag.

Mitchell showed up every afternoon until the house was painted. When the job was finished, they stepped out into the yard together to admire their work. "Looks good, doesn't it?" Megan said with satisfaction.

"It's a beautiful place," he said, meaning the entire farm.

"Thanks for your help," she said sincerely.

"It was my pleasure," he said, regretting they were finished.

A few days later Megan was in the hammock, forcing herself to relax. Doc had stopped and they were chatting. "The garden center is great and the house looks wonderful. What are you going to do next to keep from facing facts?" he bluntly asked.

"What are you talking about?" she asked, stunned.

"You and Mitchell. I never saw two more miserable

people. Do you think you'll ever be happy without him?''

''I have been for years!''

''You haven't been happy. You've been patient. I saw the way you lit up when he came back. I hadn't seen that glow in your eyes since he left,'' he stated.

''You don't know—'' she began sadly.

''No, and I don't want to know. That's your business.'' He cut her off. ''Was whatever he did so wrong that you can't ever forgive him? Forever is a long time!''

Reflecting on his words, she stared up at the sky. If she forgave him, would that make everything right? She wished it were that simple.

''He's made mistakes, but we all have. You know, I still miss my wife. Our marriage wasn't perfect, but I never loved anyone but her. If I could change the past, I would have spent a great deal more time with her. I always thought she'd outlive me. It's been mighty lonely. Is that what you want, to be alone?'' he asked.

Listening to him, Megan felt like crying. She nearly fell out of the hammock when she heard Mitchell's voice.

''Hi!'' he called from a distance. He had been looking for any excuse to come by. ''Doc, how's your lady friend?'' he asked.

Doc grinned. ''Oh, we're just friends. She's interested in this other guy, but she doesn't want him to know it.''

''Well, don't give up. I'm sure you have a lot more going for you than he does,'' Mitchell said, trying to encourage him.

''You know, you're probably right,'' Doc agreed.

Mitchell turned to Megan. "I have to go out of town next week. I thought I'd let you know."

"Your fish business?" she asked frivolously.

Doc laughed aloud, then noticed both were giving him equally dirty looks. He figured he had better escape quickly. "Well, Megan, I'll see you soon," he said, kissing her cheek.

Once Doc had gone, Mitchell started his explanation again. "I'm going to Florida on business. I wanted to ask you to come along. We'll get separate rooms, but maybe it would give us a chance to talk," he said, feeling apprehensive.

"I already told the kids I would take them to Fairy Stone next week," she said quickly.

"Oh."

"Maybe your mother would like to go with us," she said, feeling guilty, knowing he felt brushed aside.

Out of nowhere she said, "The kids were hoping you would come up for a day." She was instantly sorry she had said it. He was the last person she wanted to be with.

"If I get back early, I may drive up," he said without enthusiasm. They were going to the lake he used to take them to on vacations. And he was invited as an afterthought. Completely dejected, Mitchell picked himself up and went home.

On Monday morning, Ruth's car was packed to the roof as they headed for the lake.

About the same time Mitchell boarded a plane for Florida. He spent most of the flight thinking about the future. He had always known there was a possibility things wouldn't work out.

Megan had rented a cabin at Fairy Stone State Park. The stones found in the area resembled crosses. Megan had found a few of the stones the first time Mitchell brought her to the small lake tucked in the Virginia foothills. It was just the place to get away from it all.

Unpacking quickly, they hurried out to investigate. At the beach, Zack immediately spied the sign advertising canoes for rent. A few minutes later the kids paddled away.

Megan and Ruth stretched out on a blanket in the sun. "Megan, I know things are kind of out of whack, but don't you think you could try and talk things over with Mitchell. It breaks my heart to see what this is doing to both of you," Ruth said sadly.

Megan sighed. She didn't want to hurt Ruth's feelings, but she didn't want to discuss the matter. "You know my mother says things always work out in the end, if we trust in God," she replied.

"You know, she's right. God will work this out. I shouldn't be worrying," Ruth said, reminded that God took care of every need in His time, not hers. She began to chatter about anything that came to mind.

Megan tried to listen, but fell asleep. Some time later she was rudely awakened by Zack. He convinced her to squeeze into the life jacket Jess had been wearing and go out in the boat with him. As her son paddled along, she remembered riding on the lake with Mitchell. She tried to push the memory away. She had come here to rest, not to remember.

Megan felt torn. If she made the decision never to see Mitchell again, that would be the end of it—but she knew it wouldn't. Not as long as she was alive.

The children would always be caught in the middle. There would be holidays, birthdays, weddings, births, funerals and hundreds of other occasions when they would be forced to choose a parent. They would have

to arrange their lives around the fact that their parents
weren't together. The thought made her sad. And she
had come here to get away from her problems, not
bring them with her. She tried to enjoy the ride.

Later that evening Megan went for a walk with Zack.
They spend most of the time discussing plans for his
senior year in high school—both afraid to bring up the
subject that was really on their minds.

Finally Zack spoke up. "Mom, can I ask you something serious?"

"Sure. Ask." She knew he needed to talk, maybe
she did, too.

"Why can't you and Dad work things out?" he
asked gently.

She didn't know how to put her feelings into words.
"I'll always care about your father, but I've lost my
trust and faith in him. I believed he would always be
there for me—he wasn't," she quietly explained.

"He wasn't there for me either, but I still love him,"
Zack said, wanting to convince her. Then he thought
about what she had said. "Do you still love him,
Mom?"

She sighed as she thought back over the last few
months. "In some ways, yes, I still love him." Zack
smiled. "In other ways, no. It's not the same as it used
to be," she admitted honestly.

"But Mom, if you could talk, maybe you could find
a way to work things out. He's not a bad guy, really!
When he was at home, we all got so close."

"I know what you want," she said, hurting for them.

"Then do something," he begged.

"I can't. What's done is done!"

"Nothing is done," he said raising his voice. "You
and Dad are still married."

"We can't stay married just to please you," she said.

"Then do it because you made a promise to each other and to God," he said bitterly, angry that she wasn't trying to understand how he felt.

"Things change."

"You always taught me to put God first. To do things God's way, no matter what. Are you changing your teachings?"

"Zack, try and understand," she pleaded with him.

"No! It can't be both ways. If you and Dad get a divorce, then you're telling me vows to God don't matter and neither do His laws." Zack stared into her eyes. "Think about what you're doing, Mom. This affects all of us—not just you."

Her face dropped to her chest as the tears came.

As they walked back to the cabin, Zack put his hand on his mother's shoulder. "Mom, if there is anything you can do to get back with Dad, you should do it," he said. Not waiting for her to reply, he went in the cabin alone.

Megan sat on the porch looking up at the millions of stars. How could they work out broken vows and shattered trust?

The vacation turned out to be the getaway they all needed. They went fishing, canoeing and hiking. Zack and Jess met kids their own age and spent time with them. The family cooked out every night, then sat around the campfire talking. Despite their problems, they made peace with one another.

On Saturday night they went to the pavilion for a campground cookout. There was enough food for an army and there were games and a local band.

Zack and Jess found their friends, and left Megan and Ruth listening to the band.

A strange man stopped at their table. "Would you like to dance?" he asked Megan.

"No thanks," she declined politely.

Uninvited, he sat down with them. "How about a walk to the lake? I'm sure your sister wouldn't mind," he said to Ruth in a sickly sweet voice.

Megan glared at him. "Look, I told you no, but if you insist on bothering us, I will get very loud and you will get very embarrassed. So would you kindly leave before that happens," she threatened.

The man reluctantly left, but looked back at her, smiling. He gave Megan the creeps.

"What would you have said if I hadn't been here?" Ruth asked.

That irritated Megan even more. Then Zack came up wanting to know what she was doing talking to that man. "I think I'll go back to the cabin. I'm really not in the mood for this," she said, and left.

She followed the path back to the cabin and sat on the porch. Memories of Mitchell holding her and telling her he loved her came to mind. It was too painful to keep remembering. She got up and went to bed.

Early the next morning the Whitneys went to a lakeside church service. Praise songs were played on a guitar. The minister was an older gentleman, but he had a sharp wit and quickly gained his audience's attention. He spoke of the disappointment in life. He gave the only answer he had: Jesus Christ. "God can handle any problem, even yours," he said as his final reminder.

Just as the service was ending, Zack whispered to

Ruth, "Isn't that the guy you were dancing with last night?" Ruth smiled at him and nodded.

Megan looked at her mother-in-law, shocked. Before she could recover, the minister was standing next to Ruth. She smiled like a school girl and introduced him to her family. Then he pulled her aside and invited her to spend the day fishing with him. Ruth readily accepted.

Wanting to make the most of their last day, Megan and the kids rushed to the cabin, changed their clothes, and grabbed something to eat. The place looked like it had been ransacked as they hurried to enjoy their final hours of vacation.

Megan lay back in the sun, keeping a close eye on Jess and her friend. When she began to feel like she was baking, she went to the snack bar to get a cold soda. She leisurely resumed her watch from a chair in the shade.

The stranger from the night before stepped into her line of view, pulled up a chair across from her and sat down as though he'd been invited. "Well, here we are again," he said, sounding like they had planned to meet.

"I thought I made it clear last night I wasn't interested," Megan said, seething.

"You look like you need some company," he cooed, not at all bothered by her hostile attitude.

"Well, you're wrong. I don't," she growled.

"I've been watching you all week. You're all alone. The old lady went off with some guy. The kids are on the beach. No one else is with you. I just came to keep you company," he murmured.

His tone and the fact that he had been watching her

sent a shiver through Megan. She was about to run or scream.

"May I join you?" a man asked from behind the stranger.

"Yes!" Megan said quickly.

"Look, I was here first!" the stranger replied haughtily.

Mitchell yanked the chair out with the man in it.

The stranger was on his feet in a flash. "Who do you think you are?" he snarled.

"The lady's husband!" Mitchell answered through clenched teeth.

The man instantly turned on Megan. "You should have told me you were married," he said with false astonishment. At the moment, his only thought was to deflect a jealous husband's rage, and to escape.

Mitchell turned to Megan with his eyes full of anger and hurt. "Is this the kind of week you've had? Great example for the kids! What were you thinking, Megan?" he said, gritting his teeth.

Shocked, Megan gathered her things and started to leave. Mitchell grabbed her arm. "Wait a minute! I want an explanation."

"Let go of me," she said, struggling to get free.

"You just hold on. Who is this guy? Have you been seeing him all week?" Mitchell demanded, not even noticing the man had slipped away.

"He's just another jerk!" she sputtered, still struggling.

Zack came running when he saw his father. Mitchell loosened his grip and Megan pulled away.

"I'm going to pack. Please watch Jess," she said to Zack, and walked away.

Mitchell asked Zack, "Who was that guy with your mother?"

"I don't know. Last night there was a cookout. Gran told me some guy came up and asked Mom to dance. She refused. He sat down at the table and Mom threatened to get noisy if he didn't get lost. I guess he saw her alone," Zack said, watching his father's perplexed expression.

Mitchell knew he'd made a big mistake. "Where's your grandmother?" he asked, scanning for her and the stranger.

"She went out fishing with some old dude."

"You let her go out with a stranger, too?" Mitchell's voice rose again.

"He's a minister and about seventy, Dad. I met him last night. He's a nice guy. She'll be okay," he reassured his father. "Let's go swimming before the day is over."

"I need to change my clothes," Mitchell said.

"I'll stay with Jess," Zack offered.

Mitchell moved his car near the cabin and carried his overnight bag to the door. He knocked, hoping Megan would let him in. "Meg, it's Mitch. May I come in to change my clothes?" he asked sheepishly.

Megan opened the door and pointed to the bedroom. "I'm sorry I jumped to the wrong conclusion," he apologized. "Are you okay?" She went to the window and stared outside without answering.

A few minutes later Mitchell came out wearing a T-shirt and a swimsuit. Megan continued to ignore him.

"Remember when we came here when Zack was little," he said, trying to break the ice. "He wanted to stay in the water all the time. We took him fishing and he caught a nice bass. He was so excited, until he realized we were planning on eating his fish," Mitchell said, hoping to remind her of a pleasant time.

Megan smiled to herself. She'd been thinking about the same thing. "As I remember, we let the fish go and had a salad," she remarked.

Mitchell gently turned her to face him and brushed his knuckles across her tear-stained face. "We've had some good times. It wasn't all bad."

She glanced at him. "I know," she admitted sadly, hoping he wasn't as miserable as she was. She swallowed hard.

Just then Jess and Zack came flying in the door. Jess ran into her father's arms. "Go swimming with me," she begged, taking Mitchell's hand and leading him out.

He glanced back, Megan hadn't moved. "Come on," he coaxed her.

She shook her head. "I'm not going."

"I don't want to leave you by yourself," he said.

"I have to pack. You guys better go on while you still have time." That made Jess even more insistent.

Reluctantly Mitchell left her, not wanting to start another quarrel.

After they left, Megan looked around at the mess. She'd given up going with them to tackle this? It didn't matter, no one seemed to care.

Megan had everything packed and the cabin spotless by the time they all returned.

They decided to stop for a hamburger on the way home. "Why don't you ride back with me?" Mitchell suggested to Megan as they came out of the restaurant.

It was already dusk. Zack had been out late the night before and he'd played hard all day. "Zack's tired and your mom doesn't see well driving at night. It would be better if I drove," she said. He looked disappointed by her response.

Jess immediately volunteered to ride with her father. Ruth seconded the motion. Zack got in the car with his mother.

"I could have driven. You could have trusted me. You also could have spent some time with Dad," Zack said, once again angry with her.

She said nothing.

There was quite a bit of traffic on the highway, so Megan concentrated on the road. When she finally glanced at Zack, he was asleep.

At home, they unpacked Ruth's car first. As soon as it was empty, Ruth told them good-night and slowly drove away.

After unpacking Mitchell's car, Zack and Jess said good-night in the kitchen and started hauling their belongings upstairs.

Mitchell started out the door without a word. Megan followed him to the porch. Both stood staring into the night, not knowing what to say.

Mitchell was on edge. His mother and Jess had talked nonstop all the way back, and it had been a long, tedious drive. He was tired and not in the best of moods. It was best if he didn't say anything to Megan tonight. The mood he was in, he was liable to take her head off.

"So how was your week?" she asked lightly.

That simple question undid him. "You want to know, I'll *tell* you! I worked all week rearranging my schedule so I could come to the lake for one lousy day. I left Florida last night to get back today, and had to reroute all over the place. Then I drove two hours, straight from the airport, to be with you. And what did I get—you'd rather pack!'' he blasted her. ''I've had it with you, Megan. I have feelings too, you know.''

''I'm sorry,'' she said lamely. ''I thought you wanted to be with the kids.''

''I wanted us all to be together, as a family, but that's evidently not on your mind. I can't change the past. I don't know how to prove to you that I love you. But I really don't think it matters. You don't want me anymore. Maybe it's time—'' He stopped himself before he said what he was thinking. He gave Megan a frustrated look and went storming down the steps. He opened the car door and looked back at her standing on the porch. She hadn't moved.

When she didn't respond, Mitchell got into his car and sped away.

Chapter Thirteen

Summer came to an end and school opened. Zack knew things were getting no better between his parents. He still believed there was a chance they could get back together, but they never came near one another.

As the Indian summer days lingered, sadness encompassed Megan. She needed a new project to distract her from this bout of self-pity. Deciding a good fall cleaning was in order, she tackled a different room each day. She left the guest room until last. Opening the closet, she ran the vacuum inside to get up the dust. Something caught in the vacuum and jammed it. She shut off the machine and turned it over, pulling the offending object out.

To her surprise, it was a picture of Mitchell. He looked extremely thin, with stringy hair and a straggly beard. His eyes looked vacant and dead. She turned the photo over, so she wouldn't have to look at him. He had written on the back, *The Bottom*.

She turned it over again and studied his features. She couldn't imagine what had brought him to that place in his life. He looked so haunted and alone. If that was how far he'd gone down, he'd done a lot of climbing. For once, she felt compassion for him. She put the picture in the drawer with her special things, troubled by the photo but unable to throw it away.

Megan felt like the end was coming. Some of the heart seemed to go out of each of them as they tried to skirt around and not offend one another.

It was in the last moments, things had gone too far…it was inevitable. But ending the marriage still went against what she believed.

Zack hoped his parents would reconcile. He knew if they didn't, something inside him would die. He decided to pray about it one final time. Alone in his room, he got on his knees.

"Father God, You said to ask. Well, I have asked over and over and over. I want mom and dad together. I want my family together. We belong with each other. I can't stand to think about it any other way. Lord, I also know I can't let this be the only thing in my life. So I'm giving this care over to You. I'm putting it in Your hands. Please, Lord, help us. In Jesus' name, amen."

A foreboding feeling was in the air the day the rain began. The sky was dark and gray like a watery grave. Once the cold, hard rain began, no one wanted to go outside. The gloomy weather accentuated Megan's melancholy mood. She walked down to the river, which was still in its banks, barely. The ground was so saturated that it squished. She glanced at the garden center, knowing it would be washed away if the river flooded.

The next morning school was canceled due to flooding in low-lying areas. The river was out of its banks, catching and carrying anything in its path.

Together with her children and employees, Megan tried to save as much as possible, but they couldn't move things fast enough to keep ahead of the rising water.

Megan sent everyone to the house to move the furniture upstairs. Grabbing the hammock from the tree, she turned to find Mitchell behind her.

"Why didn't you call me?" he asked, his tone angry and accusing.

"And say what? My farm is flooding!"

The haunting look from the picture was there in his eyes. "You could have asked for your husband's help," he suggested.

"I figured you wouldn't be calling yourself that much longer," she said, watching his expression. He looked as though she'd stabbed him. She felt like kicking herself.

The river was rising before their eyes. Mitchell took Megan by the arm and led her to the house. As he came in the door, he began giving orders. "Zack, you and Jess take the pickup and go over to your grandmother's house. The rest of you guys better head on home."

"We aren't finished moving the furniture upstairs," Zack argued.

"Go now!" Mitchell commanded.

"Are you and Mom coming?" he asked, shoving a reluctant Jess ahead of him.

"Yes. Now get going!" he barked, knowing Megan would take a few minutes. Driving to the farm, the river was nearing the road in a low spot. He had heard on the radio that the bridge into town would also close soon. Mitchell knew it was time to get to higher ground—before they were trapped.

Megan thanked her employees and hurried them out. They followed Zack down the road.

Mitchell started for his car. "Come on, Meg. It's time to get out of here!"

"Go ahead. I'll be right there," she replied.

A few minutes later Megan came out with a large bag in her arms. She quickly climbed in the van. He waved her on first. She pulled out, but stopped to look back when she heard a deep groaning sound.

The greenhouse was ripped from its foundation and floated away. It hadn't gone far before it crashed into the shed, toppling it. All her years of hard work were just washing away. She couldn't believe this was happening.

Mitchell's horn sounded. Not far ahead, the water was running across the road. She started easing through the water until the van hiccuped and stopped.

Megan tried to get it started again. She rolled the window down and shoved her head out. "I'm stalled," she shouted over the rain and water.

Mitchell pulled up behind and started to push the van with his car. At last it cranked. Megan touched the accelerator and moved forward until she was across the raging current and up the incline on the other side.

Looking back, she was expecting to see Mitchell right behind her. Instead his car was in the waterway sliding sideways. It stopped when it hit the guardrail.

"No!" Megan screamed, jumping out of the van and running back to the edge of the water. "Mitchell, get out!" she hollered. He couldn't open the door, so he climbed out the window onto the hood. The swollen river was raging around him.

Her eyes left his, then returned, horrified. "Jump!"

A huge tree crashed into the car, shoving it along the guardrail. The saturated ground gave way and the roadside barrier collapsed. Suddenly Mitchell was in the savage water. He disappeared, and the car drifted away.

Frantically, Megan watched the bizarre scene. A little ways downstream she saw Mitchell surface, coughing and choking. She ran along the edge of the water trying to keep track of him.

Up ahead was a bend in the river. If she could cut across the field and get there first, she might have a chance to reach him. She took off running as fast as she could.

Managing to get ahead of him, she found a big stick. She began shouting to get his attention as she waded into the current that threatened to take her. "Swim to me!" she screamed.

With all his strength, Mitchell swam toward her. He caught the stick and she pulled as hard as she could. The flow was grabbing and clutching at both of them. Megan felt as if her arm would tear off. At last she caught his hand, and they smiled.

Unexpectedly, something under the water crashed into Megan's legs, knocking her off her feet. Immediately the current swept them downstream. They clung to one another as unknown things in the water grabbed and gouged them and as they were pulled through the turbulent, muddy froth.

Bobbing along like corks, occasionally they were sucked under. Coming up, they would gasp for air, not knowing when they would be engulfed again.

Megan loosened her grip, thinking Mitchell would stand a better chance of making it without her. He held her more tightly. Together they fought the rough water until they were suddenly taken under. It seemed they would never come up this time.

At last they surfaced, gasping for air. Mitchell saw a tree limb hanging almost within reach. With all his might, he shoved Megan toward it. She used the last of her strength to swim for it. Grabbing the branch, she held on for her life. Then she reached out for Mitchell.

He kept swimming, but he wasn't making any headway. Megan stretched out as far as she could without letting go of her lifeline. Mitchell used every bit of his strength to make it to her. Their fingertips touched. Then without warning, he was gone.

Megan searched the gushing water for some trace of him. Nothing! Anguished, she cried, "Please, God!"

Inch by inch she pulled herself up the steep embankment. Finally she was out of the bloodthirsty stream. She lay facedown in the mud, racked in sobs.

Mitchell was gone. If she hadn't looked back, he might have made it. How could she have been so stupid? "No!" A primal scream exploded from her as the heavens poured.

She began thinking maybe the rest of them hadn't made it. "Please, God, in Jesus' name, let them all be safe," she cried.

Groping and crawling, she slowly pulled herself up the slippery incline. With strength she didn't know she had, she fought her way to the top. Only then did she recognize the jutting rock. She whirled around. Behind her she could see the farmhouse.

There was no way out. She was surrounded by the river. Numb with cold, she thought of Mitchell. Her thoughts kept going back to Mitchell shoving her to the tree limb, putting her first. Then, just as their fingers were touching, he was swept away. It had been their last chance, and she'd failed him.

As darkness approached, Megan took one final look at the house before the light faded. The river had made its way to the porch. Everything else was gone. By morning the house could be gone too.

She no longer cared. All the material possessions in the world would never bring Mitchell back. She imagined Ruth, Zack and Jess wondering why they hadn't gotten there. The van would be found empty. Mitch's car would turn up somewhere. Then Mitch's body. "No! God, no," she cried.

Shaking, she crawled under the edge of the rock to find a dry spot.

Visions of Mitchell kept bombarding her. This was what hell would be like. You'd be alone, with no love, no reassurance, no God. At her favorite place, Megan felt more alone than she ever had in her whole life.

The picture of Mitch came to mind. Love wasn't supposed to fail. She'd failed miserably. She'd asked Mitch to prove he loved her. He had. He'd given his life for hers.

All her life she had been told to follow Jesus as her example, not man. She knew she failed most of the time, but she tried. Then Mitchell came home and she threw all the rules away when it came to him. *Lord, please forgive me. Jesus taught that the one without sin should throw the first stone. I threw quite a few at Mitch. I had no right.*

She brooded until she finally understood the ironic truth. Unintentionally, she had done the same thing Mitchell had. She had thrown away her family by choosing not to forgive him. She had chosen the fear of being hurt and unforgiving over Mitch.

"Forgive me, God!" she cried. The Lord's Prayer came to mind. Our trespasses were forgiven, as those who had trespassed against us were forgiven. It was too late to ask Mitch's forgiveness, but she did it anyway. "I forgive you, Mitch. Please forgive me."

Megan thought of all the things that would never be because she had been hard-hearted. If only she had forgiven him, maybe he would still be alive.

Megan tried to pray, but all that seemed to come out was "Forgive me…" over and over through the soggy night. No peace and no forgiveness came.

Darkness finally gave way to light. A mist hung in the air but patches of blue could be seen as the sky began to clear. After spending the night exposed to the raw elements, Megan was mumbling prayers, oblivious to anything else.

A rescue boat with men in yellow rain gear came by, searching the swollen river. They shouted her name as they scanned the banks for any sign of life.

In the distance, Megan heard her name. She rose, following the voices. The rescuers didn't see her until she slipped and tumbled part of the way down the path.

"Thank God!" one of the men said as they helped her into the boat. Wrapping her in dry blankets, they turned the boat around and sped away.

Megan didn't want to ask, but she had to know. "Did you find my husband?"

"Late last night, we found him lodged in the debris by the old train trestle downriver—" Megan began crying and shut out the rescuer's voice as he continued to talk. She didn't want to hear all the gory details of Mitchell's death. She felt empty.

As the boat neared the bridge, Megan noticed a

crowd with reporters and cameras. They were all being held back by the police. She searched until she spotted Zack, Jess and Ruth. Nothing would ever be the same again.

The boat came to a stop and hands reached down, pulling Megan from the boat. A cheer went up as her feet touched the ground. She was crushed in the arms of someone in yellow rain gear. She hid her face as the cameras flashed.

Even in her despair, Megan recognized the sobs of the man holding her. She pulled back to see his face, to make sure it was really him. "Mitchell!" she cried and flung her arms around him. "Thank God. I thought you'd drowned," she bawled.

Mitchell didn't answer, he just held her.

"I'm so sorry. I thought I'd killed you," she sobbed.

"It's okay," he said as they held one another and cried it out.

Jess broke free from the crowd and ran to her parents. Zack quickly followed. "Praise the Lord!" Ruth shouted as she joined the reunion.

The show was over and the crowd began to disperse. Doc came scurrying toward them. He had been at the hospital when he heard Megan had been found, but he needed to see her for himself. The past day had been one of the worst he could remember. He had even ended his cold war with God and prayed. "Thank God," he said without thinking, and hugged them all.

Against her will, Megan was taken to the hospital. After Doc patched her up, she absolutely refused to stay. Doc figured she would be better at Ruth's anyway.

Mitchell helped Megan up the stairs to the bathroom. He turned on the water, thinking a bath would ease her shaking and shivering. She hadn't said much at all. Every time she looked at him, she began crying. "Take a hot bath, it will make you feel better," he said, lifting her chin. "Everything will work out."

Megan stayed in the tub for a long time, crying. When she came out of the bathroom, she was wearing one of Ruth's flannel gowns.

Zack and Jess were sitting on the steps waiting for her. They led her downstairs to the sleep sofa as though she were an invalid. She slid gratefully between the clean sheets. Mitchell was nowhere in sight.

The phone rang constantly. Megan talked to her parents and to Cass, and briefly to Ted, assuring him everything would be fine. Exhausted, Megan laid back and closed her eyes. Everyone let her rest.

After the house was quiet, Mitchell crept to the family room and sat in a chair across from where Megan slept. While he had been trapped in the river, he had realized he had been acting like the old Mitchell again. Pushing Megan to accept him and do things the way he wanted them done. He was the one who had crossed the line. She would probably have forgiven him anything, other than being unfaithful. It was time he set her free, she had suffered more than enough. With a heavy heart, he vowed to stop hurting her.

In the morning, Megan's first move let her know she ached all over. Groggily she opened her eyes and found Mitchell asleep in the nearby chair. She knew he must feel lousy, yet he had sat up all night watching over her. Her eyes shut again.

Shortly after, she heard Ruth in the kitchen, cooking breakfast. She had so many things she needed to say to Mitch. She wished that Ruth had slept late and given them a little time to talk. But that was a selfish thought.

Megan opened her eyes again. This time Mitchell was awake. Their eyes scanned one another, each seeing the other's uncertainty.

Mitchell got out of the chair stiffly and went to look out the window. Megan watched him, grateful he was alive. Before either found the courage to speak, Ruth called them to breakfast.

The kids came bouncing down the stairs, ready to start the day. Megan slid down in the bed and pulled the covers over her head. Once again she began to sniff. The children stared at the lump in the middle of the bed, puzzled.

"Let's go have breakfast. Mom's not quite up to it yet," Mitchell said, leading the way. A few minutes later, he came back with a plate of food and a cup of coffee. He sat on the edge of the bed and peeled away the covers. "Come on, Meg, you need to eat something," he said, hauling her to a sitting position, ignoring his own aching body.

He took a bite of toast, then offered it to her. She took a bite to satisfy him. Encouraged, he continued. He didn't know what to say. She looked so dismayed. He had taken one last look back, too. She'd be lucky if the house was still standing.

Megan finally glanced at Mitchell. She wanted to talk to him, but when the tears rose in her throat, she jumped up and fled to the bathroom.

While she was in the shower, Ruth brought her clean clothes. They looked like rags. Megan tried to fix her hair but to no avail. And she had no makeup. Going downstairs barefoot, she felt like a scarecrow used past its prime.

Mitchell had everyone organized to go shopping. They were waiting for her. "Come on. We all thought we'd go shopping and get some new stuff," Mitchell announced cheerfully.

Megan glanced at herself in the hall mirror. "Just get me something to wear and whatever the kids need. I don't want to go out looking like this," she said flatly.

Megan wrapped herself in a blanket and fell asleep on the sofa. She was snatched from her slumber by knocking on the front door. She peeked out. It was one of the rescue workers from the day before.

"Hi, Megan. How are you feeling today?" he asked. "I'm Tom Pierce."

She shook hands with him. "I'm okay—a little sore here and there," she admitted as she hobbled to the sofa.

"I'm not surprised. I need to ask you a few questions for our report," he said.

Megan recounted all she could remember, leaving out the details of her night on The Hill. He rose to leave. "I brought your van."

Megan hopped up and looked out the door. Sure enough, the van was parked in the driveway alongside a rescue squad car with a man waiting for Tom.

The sight of Mitchell's car in the water flashed through her mind. "I truly appreciate all that you've done. Thank you."

"No problem," he said, stepping out the door.

Megan asked how they had found Mitchell. "He was trapped in the debris that couldn't get under the trestle. It was building up and he was wedged in. We had no idea he was there. He happened to see us and yelled for help. We would never have found him otherwise. It was kind of a miracle that we even went out there.

One of the guys said he had a feeling that we should take a look. That's the only reason we were there. A little while longer and he would have been crushed. Somebody was watching over him or praying for him or something," Tom said.

Megan nodded, fully understanding. "Tom, thank you so much for all you've done. And please thank your co-workers for me, too," she said gratefully, thinking she needed to do something for these people.

After he left, she brought her belongings in from the van. Then she went to Mitchell's room to find a shirt to replace the tattered one she had on. As she was rummaging through the dresser, she noticed the pictures lining the top. All of them were of the family, except one. In this picture, Mitchell was with an older, black man and they had their arms around one another, smiling broadly. The man looked familiar, but Megan couldn't place him. She turned her attention back to what she was doing.

When the family returned, they found Megan in the kitchen, cooking and humming to the stereo in the living room. Mitchell came in the kitchen and stopped where he was when he noticed Megan was wearing his shirt. But he said nothing. They looked at each other, but neither knew where to begin. He hurried out the back door.

Jess and Ruth were showing Megan the things they had bought. She was distracted until Jess held up a beautiful peach gown and matching robe. "I thought maybe you'd like something different for a change," Ruth said hopefully.

Megan rolled her eyes at her mother-in-law. "Now that really looks like me. This is a disaster, not a honeymoon!" Ruth chuckled because she was blushing.

"Will you all get out of here and let me finish cooking!" Megan said, chasing them out of the kitchen.

As she worked, she prayed silently. *Lord, please give me the courage to talk to Mitchell. He's been avoiding me most of the day. Nearly drowning probably brought him to his senses. I'm trusting You to work things out between us. In Jesus' name, amen.*

Chapter Fourteen

Everything going wrong made Mitchell feel like he was somehow personally responsible. To get out of the way, he went to his father's workshop in the backyard.

He hadn't been in the building since his father's death. Years before he had come here looking for his father, wanting to talk to him. Mitchell had found his father dead, slumped over a wooden wagon he had been making for Zack's fifth birthday. He had had a massive heart attack. It seemed like a million years ago.

Mitchell sat back on the stool at the workbench and reminisced. He had learned a great deal by talking to his father while he worked.

He had been crushed when his father died. He didn't think he had blamed his father for dying, but in retrospect maybe he had. He knew that was when he turned his back on God, blaming Him for taking his father from him. From that point on, he seemed to make one bad decision after another.

Yet he had left his own children without a father,

knowing how hard it had been without his. He could hardly believe some of the stupid things he'd done.

Megan drifted into his thoughts. They needed to settle things, for both of their sakes. It was no use putting this off any longer.

Mitchell picked up one of his father's tools and held it. His mom hadn't changed a thing in the workshop in all this time. She must have been lonely without her husband. And instead of helping her, Mitchell had only added to her grief. He felt depressed by all the guilt he was carrying.

Zack popped his head in the door and startled his father. "Dad, dinner's almost ready," he said, looking around. "Nice shop," he commented, reverently touching things.

Mitchell thought of all he had missed with his children. More regrets washed over him like an incoming tide.

"I took a year of woodworking. I really liked it. I wonder if Gran would let me use this sometime," Zack said hopefully.

"Maybe we could build something," Mitchell said, seeing a chance to forge a real relationship with his son, instead of the buddy-buddy thing they had now.

"That would be great! We better go in before Mom comes after us."

As soon as they got in the house, Zack asked his grandmother about using the workshop. "Use it anytime you like," Ruth said, pleased.

Zack monopolized the conversation during dinner. Jess tried to gain attention by giving her mother a detailed account of the flood. Megan listened with distracted interest. She had seen more than enough of the flood.

Jess and Zack were both making plans and settling in. She and Mitch had hardly spoken. If she didn't have a place to live or a job, he would probably be able to talk the children into living with him. Without thinking, she panicked. "You know we can't stay here indefinitely."

All eyes turned to her.

"Why can't you stay here?" Ruth asked.

"It's an imposition on you. You don't need all the extra work. We've turned your house upside down. If the house is damaged, it might take a long time to repair," she said, but stopped when she noticed the look on their faces.

"Are we homeless?" Jess wailed.

"No!" Mitchell said, giving Megan a look that said please agree with me. "When the water goes down, we'll check on the house. Until then, you'll stay here. Right, Megan?"

"That's right," Megan said, glad for Mitch's calm reassurance. "We'll all pitch in and help around here." That satisfied Jess.

After dinner Megan was still sensing her family's uneasiness. She remembered the photo albums she had stowed in the hall closet, and went to get them.

As soon as Jess saw them, she grabbed one, squeezed into the chair with her father, and started flipping the pages.

Megan settled on the sofa between Ruth and Zack as they shared a book. Jess knew the pictures by heart. She began telling her father about each picture, the way her mother used to do for her.

In the beginning Mitchell was in a lot of the pictures. Suddenly he wasn't in any. It stung, knowing he had missed these memories.

Megan followed her usual pattern, saving the wedding album for last. She opened the box and unwrapped the tissue. Jess noticed and came over, plopping down beside her grandmother. Her mother turned to the first picture, the bride coming down the aisle on her father's arm.

"You're beautiful," Zack said.

Mitchell looked at all of them huddled together on the sofa. Once again he felt left out. His eyes met Megan's.

"Come on over here and look at this with us," she said softly. Zack slid over to make room for his father between himself and his mother. Hesitantly Mitchell joined them, and Megan began turning the pages.

The last picture was of an old car speeding away with Just Married written on the back and a string of tin cans trailing behind. Mitchell glanced at Megan with his heart aching.

Megan sighed as she closed the album. "It's getting late. I'm going to get ready for bed," she declared and disappeared up the stairs, leaving the albums strewn about.

"It's not late," Jess protested. "I'm not tired!"

"Mom's tired," Zack reminded her. "Dad, could we watch TV in your room for a while?"

"Sure," Mitchell answered, his mind still on the photographs.

The children raced up the stairs to see who would get to the TV first.

"I'm pooped," Ruth admitted, and started up the stairs. She tapped on the bathroom door as she went by. "Have you got everything you need, Megan?"

"Yes, ma'am. Good night," Megan called back.

"Sleep well," Ruth said, and went to her room.

Downstairs Mitchell started collecting the albums. When he came to the wedding one, he sat down and looked through it again. They had been so young and full of hope, he thought.

He snapped the album shut, no longer wanting to dwell on the past. It was over. He would just have to learn to live with his mistakes and the consequences. When Megan came downstairs, he would just tell her he wanted a divorce and get it over with.

Mitchell pulled opened the sleep sofa, wishing he had better accommodations for her. He had offered her his room the first night; she had politely turned him down. It was a little cool in the room, so he decided to start a small fire and knock the chill off.

Mitchell was sitting on the edge of the sofa bed when Megan came downstairs. Lost in thought, his shoulders hunched, he stared into the crackling fire.

Megan walked over and stood with her back to the fireplace, warming herself, as she noted Mitch's defeated posture.

He glanced at her. She was wearing a droopy old pair of his pajamas, with the legs rolled up so she wouldn't trip over them. "I thought Mom got you a gown and robe today," he said. He had known when his mother picked it out that it wasn't Megan's style.

"She did. And it was beautiful, but..." She groped for the right words.

"It wasn't you," he finished.

Megan smiled. Then she tried to swallow the lump of fear growing in her throat. Suddenly she wanted to run back upstairs and hide in the bathroom. She took a deep breath. "I did a lot of thinking today. Nothing stays the same, does it?" she said, exhaling.

He shrugged. "I guess not."

"I'm sorry about getting you caught in the flood and everything." She tried to apologize, hoping he'd understand.

"It's okay," he said listlessly.

Megan studied him. When he first came back, he'd had an air of confidence about him. Now he seemed beaten down and defeated. She knew she was responsible for the change. She had rejected him again and again and again.

She had prayed for him every single day after he left home. Then when he came back she had let that deep, dark anger absorb her. "You know I've been wrong about a lot of things," she admitted. Then she realized it sounded as though she was pushing him to disclose his faults. She swallowed once again. Shakily, she said, "Mitchell, please forgive my unforgiveness?"

"I deserve what I got," he said flatly, knowing she was tactfully trying to find a way to tell him it was over between them.

"Only God has the right to make that decision. It wasn't my place. Forgive me?" she asked humbly. He nodded solemnly. Her chest tightened and her throat tried to close as she said in a mere whisper, "I forgive you."

Not trusting his ears, his attention snapped to her. "Wh-what did you say?"

Her head dropped to her chest. "I said, I forgive you…"

He stared at her, momentarily frozen. Then he realized it must be gratitude, not love speaking. He had saved her in that river. Now, out of gratitude, she forgave him. That was no foundation for a marriage—it was over. He was forgiven; she was grateful. Now they could be polite and friendly.

Mitchell envisioned friendly meetings, like ones you'd have with an old friend. Holiday greetings. Making small talk at their children's weddings. The thought of it made his insides grind. He got up and chucked another log on the fire, then stabbed it with the poker.

Megan scooted out of his way and slipped over to the stereo to put on a stack of old "45" records. Mitchell was deep in thought and didn't notice the music. "You promised to take me dancing," Megan said softly as she returned to his side.

Mitchell looked her over—her in his droopy pajamas. He couldn't help but smile. Then he heard the record playing.

"Dance with me," she beckoned.

"Why are you doing this?" he growled, looking tortured.

"Because I feel like dancing and you promised to take me," she said primly.

A wave of fear that she was pretending surged through him.

Megan noticed the wary look. "I never meant to hurt you," she said quietly.

"I messed up your life pretty good," he said. "You're entitled." Silence fell between them.

If the marriage was over, so be it. But Megan wasn't going to give up without one last try. She moved closer to him. "Come on, dance with me."

This time he agreed, and they began to dance stiffly. Suddenly Mitchell broke free and pretended to stoke the fire. He didn't want a second chance because of gratitude or guilt. He couldn't continue with the farce.

Megan felt rebuffed by his reaction and close to tears. Suddenly anger flared through her. Ten years of hurt and rejection surfaced. She caught his arm and jerked him toward her with every intention of telling him off. Firelight glistened on the tears on his cheeks, and he quickly turned away again.

"I can't stand this any longer," she whispered.

"I guess I knew this was coming. I can't say I blame you," he admitted painfully. "You told me not to come back if I was unfaithful. I should have listened."

She softly touched his arm. "Mitch!"

"Don't," he ordered.

"Don't what?" she asked bewildered.

"You don't want me. I'm…" He couldn't finish and hung his head in shame.

"Mitch, please don't shut me out. I know I deserve it, but please don't."

"That's nonsense."

"I was as unfaithful to you as you were to me," she admitted.

He looked at her shocked. "Who?" he demanded.

"Not who—what! I gave up on you," she admitted.

But all he'd heard her say was the word unfaithful. "Who, Megan? That Mike guy who kept hanging around?" he asked between gritted teeth, as he turned scarlet with anger and jealousy. "No, don't tell me. I don't want to know," he said, turning his back on her.

Megan felt sick. All this deception had gone too far. "I went out dancing one night while you were at the beach. With Doc," she finished evenly.

"Doc!" The name nearly choked him. Suddenly he knew it was true. Doc had given him every possible hint—short of telling him. He felt relieved and confused at the same time. But why was she telling him she'd been unfaithful?

Megan moved closer behind him and slipped her

arms around his waist, resting her head against his shoulder.

"Let go, Meg!" he said, trying to free himself.

"No, never again," she said stubbornly, holding him tight until he stopped struggling. "Mitchell Whitney, listen to me! I'm sorry it took a flood to bring me to my senses," she said unhurriedly. It was easier to speak her heart when she wasn't looking into his sad eyes. "I've been such a fool. I missed you so much. I wanted to give up when you left, but I had to go on for the kids. I missed holding you and loving you and just being with you. I prayed every single day for you to come back to me." The tears started again. "Then one day you did...but you had been gone so long. I was angry and hurt when I saw you. I didn't know *how* to take you back."

"What are you saying?" Mitch croaked, afraid to believe what he was hearing.

"Mitch, I've always loved you. I just didn't *like* you for a while," she said, trying to stop her tears. "I want a second chance," she pleaded.

Mitchell turned slowly to face her and noticed the lights were out. He listened to the familiar music. "You planned this!" he said, astonished. "You ran everyone off to bed early and had the records all set. Didn't you?"

"I guess I'm guilty, but if I waited for them to leave, we'd never be alone," she said shyly.

"You're just glad to be alive. That's no reason to make a rash decision," Mitchell said quietly.

"You know we've been second guessing each other for months. I've made enough mistakes lately. I don't want to make another one," she said. They looked at

one another, unsure how to proceed. Megan sat down
on the edge of the sleep sofa and stared into the fire.

Mitchell sat down beside her. "I know how you feel.
Did you really miss me?"

Megan looked over at him and nodded slowly. "The
whole entire time."

"You're not just grateful to be alive?"

She looked at him thoughtfully. "While we were at
the lake, Zack asked me why we couldn't work things
out. I gave him a few excuses, but I never really came
up with an answer. He told me I couldn't have things
both ways. Either I believed the promises I made to
you and God, or I didn't. I couldn't change the rules.
He was right, but I didn't want to admit it. I did a lot
of thinking while I was there. When you showed up, I
was so glad to see you, but as usual everything went
wrong. From then on I didn't do anything. I just let
things fall where they may. I was afraid of getting
hurt."

"Can we work things out?" Mitchell asked cautiously. "Can we forgive and forget, or at least put the
past behind us?"

"With God's help, I truly believe we can."

"Do you really love me, Meg?" Mitchell asked, still
sounding disbelieving.

Megan's eyes searched his. "Don't you mean, do *I*
forgive *you?*" she asked. He swallowed hard and nodded solemnly. "Yes, I forgive you," she said firmly.

"Just like that."

"Not quite. If I thought you were ever going to get
involved in any of that stuff again, I wouldn't want
you. But you've changed. You know Jesus and the love
of God shows in you." She said it from her heart.

"That's the best compliment I'll ever get," he admitted humbly.

Megan touched his face. "I love you, Mitch. You asked me to decide—I have. I want you back, until death do us part! You're my husband."

Mitchell put his arm around her, kissing her gently. An appropriate song was playing on the stereo. They stood up together. He held Megan out from him, giving her a good looking over. "You really dressed for this occasion, didn't you," he teased, brushing the tears from her eyes and taking her in his arms. She fit right where she always had, close to his heart. They wrapped their arms tightly around one another and let some of the pain escape as they danced—and joy returned to their souls.

Zack and Jess turned off the TV and started for bed. They stopped when they heard music coming from downstairs. Both crept down a few steps until they could peek into the living room. To their surprise, their parents were dancing.

The two watched soundlessly. Jess had never seen her parents look happy together before. She glanced at Zack; his eyes were glassy, as if he were about to cry.

Megan smiled up at Mitch as they danced and sang to each other. His eyes were sparkling and happy, like in the wedding pictures, before drinking took its toll. She reached up and kissed his cheek, then put hers against his. "I love you so much," she whispered earnestly.

"I was thinking we were over," he confessed, holding her closer. "Then I saw you in that outfit and I knew I had to get you back." He chuckled.

"I promised to torture you and I'm not finished yet," she teased back.

Another record began to play. They sang it together with wide smiles on their faces. Megan stretched up on her tiptoes and gave Mitch a kiss.

Zack nudged Jess. It was time for them to leave—although neither would ever forget watching their parents fall in love again.

"Thanks for saving my life again," Mitchell said quietly. Megan's eyes were questioning, but she didn't ask. There would be time later. They had a whole lifetime to tell each other everything in their hearts.

"Tell me you still love me," Megan said, needing to hear him say these words.

His eyes searched hers. "Just to tell you I love you isn't enough." He cleared his throat. "I promise to love, honor, cherish and never leave you again. I'll take care of you and be beside you. Whatever we have to face in the future, we'll do it together. I promise never to put anything before you, but the Lord God Almighty. If I make mistakes, please forgive me. If I'm hard to get along with, give me a big hug. When things seem impossible, remind me God can take care of it. I promise I'll be with you and love you, until death parts us. I'll love you for eternity, Megan, with all my heart."

Mitch caught her face in his hands and kissed her tenderly. Both had tears in their eyes as they held one another, giving each other comfort that was beyond words. Each was healing in the mercy of the other's forgiveness.

"Why didn't you tell me this before?" she asked, drawing back and searching his eyes.

"You wouldn't listen," he pointed out.

"I'm listening now," she said softly.

Their eyes held. Mitchell took her hand in his. He could feel her wedding ring against his skin. It reassured him: if she didn't still love him, she would have taken it off long ago. He smiled at her, kissing her fingertips and watching her eyes widen.

Megan slipped her arms around his neck and looked at him nose to nose. She could feel his heart racing, just like her own. "Would you kiss me again, like you did in the kitchen that day?" she asked.

Mitchell gathered her in his arms and kissed her. Yearning, she kissed him back slowly, no longer afraid of the future.

In the morning, Jess was the first to stir. She crept downstairs and found her mother and father cuddled together on the sleep sofa. "What's going on?" she asked loudly.

Mitchell and Megan sleepily opened their eyes and found their daughter staring down at them. Megan pulled the blanket over her head.

"What's on your mind?" Mitchell asked her.

"I want to go home," Jess said challengingly.

"Me, too," he agreed. They stared at one another in mutual understanding.

Jess watched her father as he got up and turned on the stereo. She wasn't expecting it when he pulled her in his arms and said, "Dance with me."

"Oh, gross!" she wailed, then giggled. Mitchell let her put her feet on his as he waltzed her around the room.

Zack came downstairs when he heard the oldies playing again. He went over to the bed and sat down beside his mother, rubbing his eyes. Megan reached over and hugged him. "Thank you for reminding me that God's way is the only way."

He smiled at her. "I knew you'd listen to Him," he said confidently. They turned their attention to Jess as she squealed in laughter. "You know this is the kind of stuff I remember. You and Dad were always laughing and happy together. I really missed it."

A fast record came on and Megan hopped up and instantly went into a crazy dance step from her past. Zack watched, then gave it a try, laughing.

Ruth came out of her room to see what all the noise was about. She stopped on the steps to watch her family doing a joyous dance. It had been so gloomy just the morning before. She was the only one who heard the doorbell.

"What on earth is going on?" Doc grumbled, having heard the loud music as he pulled in the driveway. Ruth pulled him inside and closed the door before they woke the entire neighborhood. Doc found four of his favorite people in the living room—dancing! He looked at Ruth. "What on earth happened?" But it was obvious that Mitchell and Megan had put the past to rest.

Ruth impulsively gave him a hug. "I'd say God answered a bunch of prayers."

"I think you're right," Doc agreed, having prayed for them himself. He had seen a few miracles in his time, but this was the first time he'd watched one unfold. The hand of God at work was an awesome sight to behold. Watching love renew itself was about as good as seeing it the first time. "Thank you, Lord," he prayed softly.

When Megan noticed Doc standing in the hallway, she rushed over and gave him a long hug. When she finished, the children did the same. At that moment, he finally understood—this was his family. It was God's gift to him. Megan was like the child he never had. Zack and Jess had been like his grandchildren since they were born. From the time Mitchell left until now, he had not only been needed, but wanted. He wondered if Mitchell would accept him.

"So you two finally took my advice, huh?" Doc said, trying to act smug.

Mitchell looked at the man thoughtfully. He had gotten to know him over the last few months. He could trust Doc, who was a man of his word. Mitch put his arm around Doc's shoulder. "We figured you must know what you're talking about. But I hate to take your best girl away from you," Mitchell said, and winked at him.

Doc rubbed his chin, grinning. "Like I told you. She's pretty hung up on this other guy. I figured I didn't stand a chance. But I hope she'll still have some time for an old friend."

"She will," Mitchell said, giving him a hearty hug.

Megan playfully tweaked his cheeks. "Don't give me that 'old friend' bit. You're family. And if you don't show up at least once a week, we're gonna come looking for you," she teased.

Later that morning, Megan called her parents. She decided to talk to her father. "Dad, I want to let you know Mitch and I are back together."

"I hope you know what you're doing," he said, concerned.

"I do. Come and see us sometime. You'll see," she said, knowing he wouldn't understand until he saw for himself how Mitchell had changed.

Her mother understood. She'd been expecting them

to get back together—praying for it. "Trust in God, things always work out in the end," her mother said faithfully.

"You're right. Thanks, Mom," Megan said, and hung up sighing.

Out of what had seemed to be a disaster came many blessings. With forgiveness came peace. With peace came love. With love came acceptance and joy.

That night before Mitchell fell asleep, he took Megan's hand in his. "I just want to thank God for bringing us back together." Megan's mother's words came to her mind again, *Everything works out in the end, if you trust God.* It was a lesson she would never forget.

Megan held her husband's hand and listened as he prayed. "Father God, thank you..."

Chapter Fifteen

It was a few days before the water receded enough to check the house. The road had partially washed out and the Whitneys' van bumped cautiously over the ruts and grooves. Megan touched Mitchell's arm as they crossed the place where they'd gotten caught in the flood.

As they rounded the last curve, Jess gasped when she saw only the house still standing. The strewn debris covered the land as far as they could see. It looked like a bombed-out war zone. Megan was glad she'd listened to Ted's advice and taken out flood insurance after she'd added the garden center.

Mitchell stopped the van by the house. Megan got out first and climbed the muddy porch steps ahead of the rest. She pushed open the kitchen door and looked inside. It was just the way she had left it, except for a little mud that had seeped under the door. She turned and gave them the thumbs-up signal.

A couple of places were a little damp, but there was no major damage. Zack looked around, gratefully. Jess ran to her room to see whether it had washed away.

When Mitchell came upstairs, he found Megan standing at her bedroom door, staring inside.

He wrapped his arms around his wife, then noticed the old photo of himself on the dresser. "Where did you get that picture?" he asked.

"I found it after you left." The face in the picture still haunted Megan. "I'm sorry I asked you to prove you loved me."

"Why? You proved *you* loved *me.*"

She looked at him quizzically. He took her left hand and admired her rings. "You waited for me," he replied, and kissed her cheek. "So what do we do?"

"I love this house, but your feelings are just as important as mine. We should agree on where we live," she said.

He looked at the bedroom. The furniture he had given her for their first anniversary looked like it belonged here. And even though he had never done anything to deserve it, he felt like he belonged here, too. "I'm home," he said, smiling contentedly. "I feel like starting the cleanup now!"

"Let's stay tonight," Megan exclaimed.

"There's no water or electricity," Mitch reminded her.

Megan turned and looped her arms around her husband's neck. "I want to come home. We could make a fire and eat canned beans."

"Yeah! And we could roast some marshmallows. It would be like camping out," Jess chimed in and squeezed between them.

"What'd you think, son?" Mitchell asked Zack.

Zack looked at his parents. If everything he owned had been lost, it wouldn't have mattered. He had all he needed. "Let's stay here!" He hooted.

When they heard a knock on the kitchen door, they all hurried downstairs. Ted and his family were standing outside, looking alarmed.

"I thought we'd come by and see…" Ted didn't know what to say. "You lost everything but the house."

"I didn't lose the most important things," she replied cheerfully.

"You're right," Ted agreed. "So do I need to go job hunting?" he asked.

"Not unless you're opposed to hard work," Megan said, undaunted.

Ted rolled up his sleeves. "Where do we start?"

They all pitched in and the cleanup began.

Later in the evening Mitchell and his family rode back to his mother's house. "We just came to pick up our stuff. We're moving back to the farm," Mitchell said, smiling as the kids dashed off to pack.

"Thanks for standing by me for so long," Megan told Ruth.

"I wouldn't have wanted it to turn out any other way," Ruth said.

"Are you sorry we're leaving?" Megan asked, thinking maybe Ruth would be lonely after all the company.

"Yes, but I'm glad you're all together again. That's the way it should be. Won't you stay for dinner? I invited Doc," Ruth said, looking a little flustered.

"None of this would have happened if you hadn't gone dancing with him," Mitchell teased Megan as he carried a box out.

"You wouldn't take me dancing, so he did!" Megan

called after him. "Looks like you've got yourself a date." Megan smiled smugly at Ruth.

"I'll call him and cancel," Ruth said, but she sounded disappointed.

"Doc's a wonderful man. You're a wonderful woman. Now give me one good reason why the two of you shouldn't have dinner together," Megan asked seriously.

"Well, I'd meant for it to be a family get-together," Ruth answered lamely.

"Tell Doc we ran out on you. He'll understand. Then have a nice dinner together. He'll appreciate it. He gets lonely, too."

Ruth thought about it. "It would be nice to have someone my own age to spend some time with," she said, then giggled. Megan nodded her approval.

Once the van was packed up, they said their good-byes.

"I'm glad to see you all going home together," Ruth said, standing on the porch as they filed out, hugging her and thanking her.

Megan was last. She put her arms around her mother-in-law and embraced her for a long moment. "Thanks for everything. I love you. Come to see us tomorrow. I want to hear all about your date tonight."

Ruth blushed and waved until they drove out of sight. "Thank you, Lord," she said, grateful for answered prayers. Then she hurried inside to set the table for two.

At the farm that night it was candlelight and carry-out food. They spent the evening sitting around the fireplace, talking. At bedtime they climbed the stairs together, each carrying a candle. It looked like a ceremony.

Megan went into the bathroom to brush her teeth. She poked her head into the bedroom with her mouth full of toothpaste. Mitch was sitting on the side of the bed staring at the crumpled picture of himself. She rinsed her mouth and went to him.

"I never thought I'd get to come home again," he said quietly, handing her the picture. "I didn't think you'd ever forgive me."

"I really wanted to hate you. I tried. Then I'd look at Zack or Jess. If I hated you, it was like hating them. One of the things I love most about our children is their likeness to you."

She took his face in her hands and looked into his eyes. "When I was alone on The Hill, I understood how alone you must have felt. I really thought you'd drowned. All I wanted was another chance. The same thing you wanted." She kissed him softly.

He cast off his dismal mood. "We don't need to keep looking back, do we?"

"God gave us a second chance. It's up to us what we do with it," she said, and put her arms around him.

The Whitneys quickly settled into the house and started rebuilding Meadow Flowers. Ted came up with some great ideas. He was anxious to get the business going again. Megan knew this would have been the perfect opportunity for Ted to leave and open his own business, but he stood by her. She intended to reward his faithfulness.

Mitchell finally found the courage to ask his family to come and see him at work. Ruth and Zack already knew Mitchell's well-kept secret, but he wanted to reveal his new occupation to Megan in person. She hadn't even considered that he was involved in anything other than the "sea" business, and he let it stay that way until he was ready to tell her.

Mitchell was scheduled to speak at a local hall one evening, but he simply told Megan he had been asked to give a speech to the community on his business. "This would be a good chance for you to get a glimpse of my new fishing career," Mitchell told his wife, trying not to laugh.

"That's great," she said, giving him a big hug.

As they arrived at the auditorium that evening, Megan noticed the sign: See Life. "They spelled it wrong," she commented to Mitchell as they entered. He chuckled to himself. He seated his family near the front, excused himself and went backstage. The auditorium was almost full.

At seven o'clock an old, black man came on the stage. He introduced himself as Paul Ruston. He bowed his head and said a short prayer.

Megan thought this was unusual. And she thought the man looked vaguely familiar. Then she remembered: he was the man in the picture on the dresser, the one who had dropped off Mitch's belongings that Sunday.

Paul Ruston began talking. "I met Mitchell Whitney on the street many years ago on a cold, wintry night. My life has never been the same since. He is one of my closest friends. I love him like a brother. Meet my friend Mitchell Whitney, the head of See Life," he said.

Mitchell came on stage with a small round of applause, mostly from his family and a few stray friends. He was obviously nervous.

Mitchell glanced at his family and smiled weakly. "When Ruston says he met me on the street, he's being very generous. Actually, I was lying in the gutter when he found me. I'd passed out and landed there, dead drunk," Mitchell said.

"You see, I'd given up on life. I hadn't consciously set out to hurt anyone, but in my inebriated blur I did a lot of things I never meant to do. And I was very much ashamed of myself."

Mitchell took a deep breath and expelled it. "Life was just too hard. I wanted things easy. Things had gotten too tough and I wanted to give up…die. So I sat on a curb with snow coming down, a freezing wind blowing, and drank and drank and drank until I passed out. Then I fell into the gutter. It seemed to be a fitting end for a loser like me. I figured no one would notice me there. The snowplow would just scrape me up with the rest of the trash.

"But Paul Ruston noticed. He picked me up and dragged me home with him. I was so far gone, I didn't even know what was happening. I was sick from exposure and malnutrition. I was also an alcoholic. Paul tells me I was very unpleasant when I began to come around. He stuck a mirror in my face and told me to take a good look." Mitchell involuntarily shuddered. "I didn't like what I saw."

Megan listened to him, dumbfounded.

Ruston put a copy of the picture Megan had found on the screen behind Mitchell. "This was how I looked when I finally bottomed-out. Nothing really mattered to me anymore. Or that's what I kept telling myself. Paul asked me if there was someone he could call— family or a friend. Someone who loved me. I lied and told him there was no one. Although a face flashed through my mind.

"Now most of us have at least one person who will love us, regardless. I knew my mama loved me." He smiled at Ruth. "But that wasn't the face. The face I saw…I wasn't sure she loved me anymore." His eyes settled on Megan. "I saw the face of my wife.

"I'd left her several years before. At the time, she was in the hospital with complications from the pregnancy of our second child—" He glanced at Jess. "I didn't want to face my problems, much less her. When she told me I had to make a choice between her and my current life-style, I did. I ran…and ran…and ran," he admitted.

"I kept running until there was no place left to go. I couldn't get away from myself. I was the problem. I was an alcoholic," Mitchell confessed, "and I no longer cared whether I lived or died."

"'Call her,' Paul kept saying. 'I can't,' I told him. But he kept at me and I finally called. She answered on the second ring. I listened to her say 'hello' three times." Mitchell closed his eyes and remembered Megan's irritated voice when he didn't say anything. "Just hearing her voice helped, but I knew I couldn't face her. I was worse than when I'd left her. I hung up without saying anything.

"Paul asked me if I thought she'd give me a second chance. I told him she already had, so many times I'd lost count. It was too late. Paul calmly agreed with me. He didn't think she'd take me back, either, in the state I was in. He asked me whether if I could change for her, I would."

Mitchell sighed. "I'd tried. Many times before. I just

couldn't do it. It was too hard. It was easier to just give up and give in." He dropped his head in shame.

Paul Ruston knew how difficult this was for Mitchell. This was the hometown crowd. People he would have to face as long as he lived here. But Megan was here. This was his public confession to her and to his family. He went over and put his arm around Mitchell. "I know you couldn't change. Not on your own. But I had a friend who I knew could help you. I knew he could help you because he helped me out of that same gutter," he said softly.

Mitchell lifted his head and looked at his friend. Paul nodded at him, giving him a look that said, *You can take it from here.* "Paul began to tell me about his friend," Mitchell began again. "He told me how his friend helped him get off drugs. He said his friend had been with him all the time and never left him alone. The man sounded wonderful! Almost too good to be true. I told him I wanted to meet this friend of his. I needed someone like him to help me straighten out my life.

"Then Paul told me his friend's name was Jesus Christ. I went berserk. I had been dragged off the street by a do-gooder, religious fanatic. I got up and walked out of his house. 'You'll never know peace until you meet Him,' Paul called after me.

"I walked the streets for hours. I didn't want to go back. I didn't want to go forward. All I wanted was peace. I needed to find a way to get out from under the burden of guilt, fear and disappointment I felt every moment I was alive. Once more I began to think I wanted to die," he said.

"I passed guys sleeping on park benches; they looked just like me. I saw others digging through trash

bins for something to eat. I'd done that, too. A carload
of drunk kids nearly ran me down and kept going. The
thought flashed through my head, *In a few years they
could be in my place.* I was a homeless person. This
was the life I had chosen.

"I began to weep as I kept wandering. I found myself in front of Paul's house again. The man was offering me a chance to get out of the gutter.

"Hesitantly, I went to the door and knocked. He let
me in without saying a word. Then he sat me down
and told me in vivid detail about his former life. It
sounded like a carbon copy of mine. He had also chosen to leave his family in pursuit of himself.

"I didn't want to listen to him. He'd been there. He
would make me face what I'd become. I couldn't lie
to him, he already knew me for what I was. But I
realized then that even though I no longer had any
reason to live, I didn't want to die. So I listened to
him." The audience was silent.

"Paul brought to light many things my parents and
wife had tried to tell me. But I never listened before. I
wanted life on my terms. My terms brought me to the
end of the road. I'd given up my wife, children, mother,
home, friends, health—and even my car." Teens in the
audience chuckled.

"The only things I owned were the clothes on my
back, a Bible my mother had given me, and a picture
of my pregnant wife holding our son. Everything else
I had traded for a drink.

"Before I met Paul, I never realized how far I'd
fallen. He asked me what I really wanted." He looked
at Megan. "I wanted to see my wife. I wanted to see
my children. I wanted them to love me. I loved them.
I wanted a second chance. At times we all need a sec-

ond chance," he said, pausing to scan the audience. Many heads were nodding in agreement.

"That night, I got on my knees to pray. Before, I'd never felt I needed to kneel before anyone. Paul knelt with me. We prayed. I told Jesus about my messed-up life. By the time I finished telling Him my sins and sorrows and He finished giving me His love, I had what I'd been searching for: peace. It's the kind of peace only God can give, because it's making peace with God.

"No, all my problems weren't instantly solved. Jesus didn't change all my bad habits and take away all my wrong desires, but knowing Him changed my heart. And with His help, I began to change myself. I wanted to do it, for Him. After all, He'd died for me," Mitchell said, peaceful satisfaction in his voice.

Megan started digging for a tissue, and passed a few out when she noticed all the wet eyes. Hearts were touched by God's love and forgiveness for this man.

"I changed for Him," Mitchell continued. "It took a long time. I felt so unworthy, but God had a plan. At first, I worked with Reverend Paul. I helped him with his ministry, staying under his protective wing. Then the time came when I knew God wanted me to go solo. I was invited to speak to a church youth group. The pastor wanted me to tell them my life story. I thought to myself, *Why would anyone want to hear my story?* I was afraid to do it, but I spoke because I knew that's what God wanted me to do.

"I started telling them how I'd messed up my life and deserted my family because I'd chosen the easy path. I spelled out how alcohol can blind you from what's going on. You no longer see or think clearly, but for those of us with problems that's fine. We don't want to face our problems or admit we have weaknesses, so we hide them in a bottle. Thinking we won't have to deal with them. 'Til one day we all come to the end of the road. And when we get there, nothing is left but life or death.

"The road to God isn't easy. And every person has to choose to follow that road for themselves. No one can do it for you. It's your life—only you have the right to decide where you will spend eternity. Choose wisely, because you will have to live with your decision forever. It took me ten years to make my way back home. It wasn't easy, but it was definitely worth it." Mitchell paused.

"Tonight, since this is the hometown crowd, I'll tell you a little more. Some of you may remember, there was a youth conference in Roanoke and I was one of the speakers. To my surprise, my son came to that conference. A teacher who knew I'd be there offered my son a deal he found hard to resist. Neither of us knew the other would be there. After ten years my boy still knew me. He came up after the meeting and introduced himself. I was overwhelmed. My son still loved me." Mitchell's voice trembled.

Megan looked at Zack. He had known all along. Zack offered his hand to his mother. She took it and squeezed.

"I told God I wanted to come home, but when it got down to it, I was afraid," Mitchell confessed. "So I made a deal with myself. If I went to that conference and didn't see any of my family, I would know I shouldn't come back.

"God had other plans. He brought my son to that conference. And my son begged me to come home. He still wanted me. We talked for a long time that night.

Then I sent him home and left town the next morning. But my boy loved me, I had to see him again. I *needed* to see him again.

"Over the years, I've moved from place to place telling my story. Hoping to keep some kids from taking the same path I took. Along the way I've met a lot of wonderful people who have also led destructive lives and been healed by the grace of God. And a while back, I was asked to organize a network of people willing to spread the message of God's love and forgiveness by telling their personal stories. I call this organization See Life, because before I knew Jesus, I was lost—and now I see. I tried to get the organization going while on the road, but I knew I needed a home base to efficiently run See Life. And in my heart I kept hearing my son, begging me to come home.

"God was telling me it was time to face the past. I moved back here and set up an office, and the project has been blessed with wonderful success. We have put speakers and groups together all over the country. And before long, we'll grow to the international level." Mitchell usually ended his talks at this point, but there was now a new chapter to his story.

"Would you like to know what happened to my family?" he asked the crowd with a smile. There was thunderous applause.

"Well, I finally got the courage to visit my wife. She was shocked to see me. But you know, even though she was still wearing those two rings I had put on her finger years ago, I had to get beat half to death and almost drown before she'd take me back." The group laughed.

Then Mitchell got serious. "I'd gladly die for her— that's how much I love her. And she'd do the same for me." He looked directly at Megan. "That's the proof, to be willing to die for what you believe and those you love. I wouldn't die for alcohol, though it nearly killed me. But I would give my life for someone I love."

Megan began to weep silently. Zack put his arm around her and Jess squeezed closer to her.

Mitchell looked at the faces in the room. "Some of you are on the wrong road. You're drinking or taking drugs. It seems good now, because you can forget your problems for a while. But eventually, it will own you and you'll be miserable until it ends…one way or the other. Life…or death. Think about where you want to spend eternity. The choice is yours.

"I traded my family for alcohol. Then I gave my life to Jesus and He gave my family back to me. I'd like to introduce them to you. Ruth Whitney, my mother. My son, Zack. My daughter, Jessica." Each one came on the stage and gave him a big hug, and the audience clapped enthusiastically. Then he looked over to where Megan sat alone. His voice cracked as he said, "My beloved wife, Meg."

Megan ran up the stage steps and into his waiting arms. At this point almost everyone in the place had tears in their eyes. Paul took over the rest of the service. He asked those who would like to meet his friend, Jesus, to come to the front. Many came and gave their hearts to Jesus.

As the service closed, a round of applause went up for the speaker. Mitchell Whitney, a prodigal son, who had come home to face his past in hopes of making the future better. The Reverend Ruston sang "Amazing Grace," and closed the service with a prayer. "Father God, I ask that You bless Mitchell and See Life and the city of Bedford for giving a hometown boy their support. May Jesus always reign in Bedford. Bless those who choose Jesus tonight. Help us to love and encourage one another. Let us all leave this place with God's blessing. In Jesus' name, amen.''

Once the service was over, Mitchell gave Megan a quick hug before the audience swarmed the stage. Megan felt someone tap her on the shoulder, and turned to find Mr. Carlyle. ''Mr. Carlyle, this is a surprise,'' she said, trying not to look shocked.

''Mrs. Whitney, I owe you an apology. I came here tonight because I heard See Life was some sort of crazy cult involving drugs. I'm on the city counsel and we were ready to run this business out of town on hearsay. I never made the connection that the man behind See Life was your husband. I came tonight expecting to run a charlatan out of town. Instead I found myself asking for forgiveness,'' he admitted unsteadily.

''You warned me, but I wouldn't listen. I thought I could play my games and my wife would take it. She didn't. She left me about four months ago. She says she never wants to see me again. I've never been so miserable. You told me to spend time and effort on my wife. I laughed at you. I thought you were a fool, wasting your time waiting for him.'' He looked over at Mitchell. ''But it turns out I was every bit as big a fool. I threw her away—now I want her back.''

''I'm truly sorry, Mr. Carlyle,'' Megan said, taking him by the arm and leading him over to Mitchell. He was just finishing a conversation as they came up. ''Mr. Carlyle, this is my husband, Mitchell. He's the best person I know to tell you how to get your wife back,'' she said, smiling at Mitch.

Megan's sister, Cass, came up to her in tears. Her son, Brian, was standing beside her. ''Cass, what's wrong?'' Megan asked. Her sister wasn't prone to tears.

"Oh, Megan, you have to forgive me…us.'' She continued to cry.

"Forgive you, for what?'' Megan asked. Brian was staring at the floor as though he hoped it would open up.

"Mitchell asked us to come. Hasn't he told you what happened?'' Cass asked.

Megan glanced at Mitchell. He was still in heavy conversation with Mr. Carlyle. "What happened?'' she asked.

Cass looked at Brian. "Would you like to tell her?''

He nodded solemnly. "It was all my fault. I didn't mean for him to get hurt.''

"Hurt? Who? What are you talking about?'' Megan asked, confused.

"Mitchell. He found out I was in trouble with some drug suppliers. I owed them money and I didn't have all of it. He went with me to talk to them. They decided to teach me a lesson, and held me while they beat him,'' Brian cried. "I'm so sorry. I never meant for all this to happen. I tried to kill myself. Mitchell and Zack got me into a drug rehab program. I begged them not to tell you. I couldn't face disappointing anyone else.''

Megan hugged him firmly. "I guess they thought you'd tell me when the time was right,'' she said. "I love you, Brian. If I can do anything to help you, just tell me. How are you doing now?'' she asked, wiping the tears from his eyes.

He nodded positively. "Good, really good. Aren't you mad at me?'' Megan hugged him again. "You know, I never understood why Mom was so against Mitchell. He's a nice guy,'' Brian said.

"Well, maybe she'll change her mind," Megan said, looking at her sister.

"I knew he'd gotten involved in drugs," Cass admitted, "but I didn't want anyone to know. I was ashamed. I had this image of my family I needed to uphold. You were the last one I wanted to know my family wasn't perfect. My pride couldn't take it. So I kept pretending nothing was wrong. Then it all fell apart the night Mitchell was beaten. So I decided to blame him," Cassie admitted. "But Brian wouldn't let me lie to you and tell you Mitchell was at fault."

"Would you have told me the truth if Mitchell had died? Or would you have let the secret go to the grave with him?" Megan asked.

"I don't know. I've always been jealous of the way you two felt about each other," Cass said, staring at her sister.

"Cass, I don't have anything you can't have. Only God knows all the problems Mitchell and I have gone through. But you have to care more about the ones you love and less about what people will think," Megan said.

Jess came up and slid her arm around her mother and her aunt. Megan looked at Jess, then back to Cass. "You need to set some things straight with her," Megan told her sister. Cass nodded and led Jess off to the side to talk.

"Mitchell's really something," Brian said, watching his uncle at work.

Megan looked over at her husband. "Yeah, he's something special all right."

"You know, I never remember you saying anything bad against him—not the whole time he was gone." He sounded awestruck.

"I'm blessed to have him back," Megan said. She noticed Mitchell shaking his last guest's hand. A few minutes later Jess and Cass came back, smiling.

"I was hoping both of you would come tonight," Mitchell said to Brian and Cass as he joined the group. He waited to see Cass's reaction.

"You know, Mitchell, I guess I never gave you much of a chance. I'm sorry for everything," Cass said, offering a peace treaty.

"It's okay. God worked it all out for the best," said Mitchell, smiling.

Before Brian left, he hugged his uncle and thanked him for all his help. Jess went to find her brother and grandmother.

Mitchell turned Megan to him. "So what do you think of *S-E-E* Life?" He spelled it out for her.

"I guess I'm beginning to see." She laughed.

"I want you to meet Paul," he said, leading her to his old friend. "Paul, this is Meg."

Paul Ruston held out his hand. Megan ignored it and gave him a big hug, saying, "I don't know how to thank you enough. God bless you."

"You know Mitchell talked about you so much, I feel like I already know you," he said, grinning. "It was kind of you to keep him. He owns this old house we're renovating for homeless families. We didn't expect that family to just show up, but they needed a place to stay. I was just getting his stuff out of the way, not expecting him to come back, but you sure put him to the test." He laughed.

"I just wanted him to know I was serious," she said, blushing, remembering Ruston ducking past her in the yard. "I guess you two are working together?"

"You didn't tell her anything, did you!" Paul said

frowning at Mitchell. "I'm getting pretty old. So I decided to retire as a pastor. But retirement is pretty boring if you haven't planned to do something else. I was just knocking around the house and going out on cold nights looking for guys in the gutter. Not much of that going on in warm weather, you know."

Megan laughed; she could tell he was quite a character.

"Mitch called, asking if I'd help him with his work. I packed up and caught the first plane out of there. I don't have time to retire now. I never found my family, but I refuse to give up the search," he said.

"I would consider it an honor if you would come to dinner tomorrow night," Megan said.

"What time?" Ruston asked immediately, knowing he was going to like this lady.

They all walked to the empty parking lot together, talking. Ruth was exhausted, but overjoyed as they drove her home. Zack and Jess hugged their parents and went to bed as soon as they came in the door.

It was a beautiful night with a full moon. Mitchell led Megan to the porch swing to enjoy the view. They were quiet for a while, listening to the night sounds and their own thoughts.

Mitchell waited patiently, knowing Megan would want some answers. Finally she asked humbly, "Why did you let me believe...think...assume you were in some sort of fish business?"

"I knew sooner or later the truth, all of it, would come out. But to come home and just blurt it all out—I couldn't do it. I didn't know how to tell you. So I just let things come out in their own time."

"But Brian! Why didn't *you* tell me? I thought you'd gotten in trouble again."

"With this job comes confidentiality. I had to respect his wishes. I'm sorry, but what was I to do?"

"Keep your word," Megan admitted reluctantly. "But why didn't you tell me about See Life?"

"I guess because I wanted you to believe in me, not in what I do," he said.

It made perfect sense to her. "I don't know what to say, Mitch."

"You don't have to say anything."

"Yes, I do," she said.

He pulled her closer, holding her in his arms. "What do you have to say, sweetheart?"

She thought before she answered. "I'm very proud of you. You make me feel…blessed. You said things tonight that deeply touched my heart. I never realized how hard it was for you to come home."

"Tonight was rough. I wasn't sure I could admit my faults to all of you. But you never gave up on me. I don't know how I would have handled that. I needed for you to still love me, to forgive me," he revealed.

"But I did give up, the night you told me…" She hung her head, ashamed.

"No, you didn't. You talked to me the next night. I thought you had given up on me when I came back from the beach, though."

"Why, because I told you I went out?"

"No, because you didn't have your rings on. When I first came back and saw those rings, I knew I still had a chance. But when you took them off, I didn't know what to do," he admitted.

"So you came over and helped me paint!" Megan teased.

"You know, I actually hated it when we finished."

"Me, too," she said, snuggling closer.

"You did? Why didn't you say something?"

"It was too much of a risk. I was afraid of making a mistake—just like you said."

"So instead of risking talking to me, you went into a flooded river after me!"

"Sometimes it takes a life-or-death situation to make you realize what life is all about. You already knew that, didn't you?" she said, putting her arms around his neck.

He hugged her for a long moment. "Help me?"

"Help you what?"

"I need you with me, to give me moral support. It's hard to pour your heart out, then go to an empty motel room." His eyes searched hers. "I know you don't want to leave Jess. I don't either. So we can work around that. I also know you have a business to run. I'll work around that, too. I just want us together when I go out on speaking engagements. We make a great team. You don't know how wonderful it was to know you were there tonight."

Megan's eyes never left his. "You're the best thing that ever happened to Jess. Ruth will help us. I've wrapped my life around my business for years. The pay is good, but it doesn't love me. Ted's past due for a big promotion and a lot more responsibility. My place is with you. Everything else will work out, if we trust God to help us."

Mitchell forgot the rest of what he was planning to say as he tenderly kissed his wife. Megan whispered, "I love you," and kissed him back.

The next evening Ruston, Ruth and Doc came over for dinner. As they joined hands at the table to say the blessing, Mitchell knew their hearts were together as well. The conversation around the table was lively as everyone tried to get in their say. After dinner it was still light, so they all decided to go for a walk. The remains of the dirt road were still there, so they headed toward the river.

Before long, Jess and Zack took off running, playfully chasing one another. Megan remembered that a few months before she'd been thinking everyone was leaving her, and that she would be all alone. Then she had dared to trust God and He had brought them all back—and even added some. *From now on Lord, You lead and I'll follow.*

Reverend Ruston looked over at her and smiled, almost as though he had heard her thoughts.

As Mitchell watched his loved ones, he felt the depths of God's mercy. He knew he deserved none of this, but he gladly accepted God's gift. Mitchell then voiced his heartfelt belief. "At the end of our lives, God's love and what we have done with it is all that will really matter."

* * * * *

Dear Reader,

I never thought I'd be writing a romance novel. Life has a way of taking unexpected turns. As my children began reaching their teens, then going on to college, I realized I was losing my position as a full-time mother.

I prayed, seeking direction for my life. I kept remembering the words of a nun I had in elementary school. "Everyone has at least one good book in them and should write at least one book in their lifetime." Now, I was sure she was talking to the rest of the class, not me. Yet all these years later I was reminded of her statement.

I sat down with a notebook and pen one night to see if I could write a short story. I stopped several months later. *Two Rings, One Heart* came from that short story. The story really touches my heart. I still can't read it without crying.

The story of Mitchell and Megan depicts a marriage that has gone wrong. Broken vows and desertion lead Megan to believe that Mitchell can never change. But the power of God's love can overcome their problems. When their hearts are willing to forgive, as God forgives, they can be healed of the hurts they have caused one another.

I hope you enjoyed reading *Two Rings, One Heart*. I would love to hear from you. You can write to me at Steeple Hill or P.O. Box 471, Ridgeway, Virginia 24148.

Martha Mason

Take 3 inspirational love stories FREE!

PLUS get a FREE surprise gift!

Special Limited-time Offer

Mail to Steeple Hill Reader Service™
3010 Walden Avenue
P.O. Box 1867
Buffalo, N.Y. 14240-1867

YES! Please send me 3 free Love Inspired™ novels and my free surprise gift. Then send me 3 brand-new novels every month, which I will receive months before they appear in bookstores. Bill me at the low price of $3.19 each plus 25¢ delivery and applicable sales tax, if any*. That's the complete price and a saving of over 10% off the cover prices—quite a bargain! I understand that accepting the books and gift places me under no obligation ever to buy any books. I can always return a shipment and cancel at any time. Even if I never buy another book from Steeple Hill, the 3 free books and the surprise gift are mine to keep forever.

103 IEN CFAG

Name	(PLEASE PRINT)	
Address	Apt. No.	
City	State	Zip

This offer is limited to one order per household and not valid to present Love Inspired™ subscribers. *Terms and prices are subject to change without notice. Sales tax applicable in New York.

ULI-198   ©1997 Steeple Hill

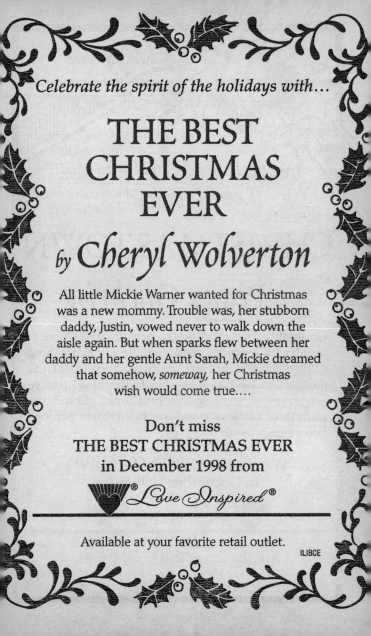

Available in December 1998 from
Love Inspired®...

CHRISTMAS TOWN
by Peggy Gilchrist

Grumpy businessman Jordan Scoville never understood why everyone made such a big deal about Christmas. And he was positively appalled at the prospect of helping lovely Joella Ratchford restore Christmas to their festive little town. Could the warmth of her love ever turn this resident Scrooge into a true believer?

Watch for CHRISTMAS TOWN
in December 1998 from

ILICT

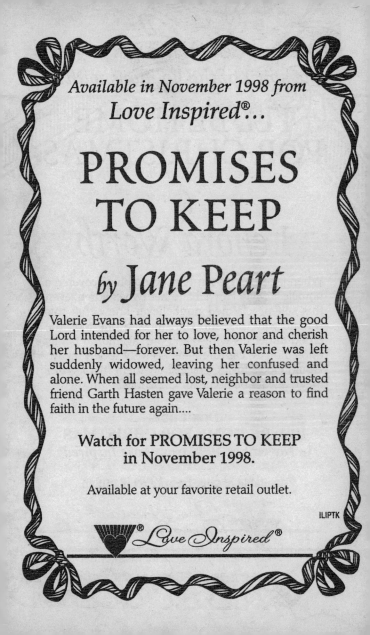